How I Became a
Teenage
Survivalist

A novel by

Julie L. Casey

Amazing Things Press

Book design by Julie L. Casey

This book is a work of fiction. Any names, characters, or incidents are the product of the author's imagination and are used fictitiously. Any resemblance to actual events, locales, or persons, living or dead is purely coincidental.

ISBN 978-0692399750

Printed in the United States of America.

For more information, visit

www.teenagesurvivalist.com
or
www.amazingthingspress.com

For my four adventurous sons
Andrew, Sean, Jack, and Todd,
who love a good story with a mix of cowboys,
survival, and ingenious inventions.

Chapter 1

I hate to write. Well, not exactly. I like to put words together in interesting ways, to lay them down and roll them out like a newly paved road stretching into the distance, daring you to follow wherever it will lead. Writing is like that for me – when I start, it draws me along, showing me new places and giving my brain interesting challenges until I come to the end of the story. Most times, I don't know where my writing is going to lead me, so it's always an adventure. At least, until the day the power grids failed and I couldn't type on the computer anymore. What I hate, to be precise, is writing my stories down on paper.

My mom says that, even though we can't go to school anymore, there's no reason to put a halt on our education and she's right. I got kind of bored in the weeks after PF (Power Failure) Day. There only so many chores to do, so many books to read, so many conversations to have, especially when you live in the country like we do. Here, your closest neighbor lives two miles away and the closest kid your age lives over five miles away. There are no phones, no TV, no video games, no lights to read by at night, not to mention no refrigeration, no microwave, and no cars after the gas ran out. No life, really; well, not the kind we were used to anyway.

Mom said that I should keep this journal and write down all that happened on PF Day and afterward, because when we eventually get the power back on like we did for a while a few months after PF Day, no one in the future will understand how bad it was unless they read an actual account of it. She said I could use this as a Language Arts assignment. So, that's why I'm writing this with a pen, on paper - ugh.

I am the second of three brothers. Mom thought it would be cool to name us in alphabetical order, so my older brother is Alexander, I'm Bracken, and my little brother is Calvin. Mom always jokes that if she'd had another kid, she would have named it Done.

I don't especially like my name. I mean, it sounds kind of cool and all, but it means "fern." *Fern!* Do I look like a *fern*, Mom? Dad, why didn't you step in here? Seriously, there are plenty of cooler names that start with B – Baron, Beck, Blade, or how about

Bond? (Notice how I put them in alphabetical order for you, Mom.)

As for my older brother, everyone calls him "Alexander the Great." My parents and grandparents (and Alexander) think he's "the golden boy," nearly perfect in every way, but I know the real Alexander, and I can tell you he's not so great. He's eighteen and two years older than I am, but you'd think he was a generation ahead, the way he acts toward me, all condescending and patronizing.

My little brother, Calvin, who is two years younger than I am (you can do the math), acts just like his namesake from the cartoon Calvin and Hobbes. He's really smart but kind of ornery and annoying. He's cool, though. I get along with him a lot better than I do with Alexander. But now we're all stuck together at home, thanks to the sun.

I was fifteen when the first solar superstorm wreaked havoc on our lives. It was November 1st and I was at school, trying to concentrate on what the geometry teacher was trying to teach us. I couldn't quite make my brain behave – it kept wandering away on its own adventure about the girl in the desk in front of me, Silky Henderson. Man, was she hot!

It didn't help that she was wearing a short sweater and low-cut jeans, or that she kept leaning forward in her chair, making the sweater inch up her back, then sitting up straight and hiding her skin like a teaser for the Promised Land. (See? There it goes again. My brain, that is.)

I vaguely remember at one point the vice-principal coming in during class and talking to the teacher, Mr. Andresen, in a low, kind of hurried voice. I might have been able to hear what he was saying if I had tried to listen, but there was Silky's back, again, as she leaned forward to take advantage of the break in the lecture to do a little flirting with the guy in front of her.

Even if there hadn't been a tease going on right in front of me, I probably wouldn't have listened to the conversation at the front of the room – "adult" talk used to bore me. I wish I had listened that time, though. Maybe I would have had a little jump on what was going to happen next.

Fourth hour (and the exquisite torture of Silky's skin) was almost over when, all of a sudden, there was a loud explosion in the distance. Then, all the lights flickered out, some popping and sparking before they went dark. Everyone put their hands over their heads and some of the girls screamed as we looked around in confusion.

It wasn't completely dark inside the classroom since there were a series of tall windows on the outer wall to let in daylight, but it was a little weird not to hear the faint hum of the fluorescent lights or the whir of the teacher's computer and docucam. It's funny how you don't even notice things like that until they're gone.

Everything was silent for several seconds except for faint echoes of the explosion and other unidentifiable bangs and pops from outside. It seemed like everyone froze for a couple of seconds. Then we all started talking in a rush, like we all had something in our mouths that we had to spit out immediately or we would choke on it. We all knew something serious had happened. Our first thought was of another grain elevator explosion. It was harvest season and there were thousands of tons of grain being loaded into the elevators from trains and semis. One had just exploded a few days before in a neighboring community, killing six people. We were all worried because everyone in our school knew someone who worked at the elevators or hauled grain there.

Mr. Andresen managed to settle us

down, telling us that the power outage would be temporary and that the explosion was most likely a transformer. Some of the, shall I say, "less intellectual" among us thought he meant the robots from outer space that change into vehicles. One doofus (I won't say his name in case he or his family read this) even said, "Cool! I knew they were real!" We all had a good laugh at his expense.

"No," Mr. Andresen explained, "It was an electrical transformer at the power station that has probably blown because we have just experienced the effects of a huge coronal mass ejection from the sun."

Mr. Andresen was also a part-time science teacher who liked to throw around scientific words like that. When he realized nobody had any idea what he was talking about, he explained that there had been a huge storm on the surface of the sun that had sent magnetically charged particles to Earth, which had caused enormous power surges in some electrical plants. He also mentioned that scientists studying the sun's activity had known it was coming for several hours, and that Vice-Principal Cox's quiet message earlier in the period had been a warning.

Nice of them to tell us!

By now, chaos had erupted outside. We could hear sirens and shouting, so we all crowded the windows to see what was going on. People were lining the streets in our small town, pointing up at sparking power lines and the tops of telephone poles that were engulfed in strange, blue flames. In the distance, we could see a huge cloud of black smoke rising from the power plant and all three of our town's volunteer fire department trucks already racing toward it.

Later on, we would find out that even three of the four huge windmills that help supply our town with electricity had caught on fire, although they burned out quickly. People reported being shocked by their cell phones, and some of the newer, more expensive vehicles – the ones with all the gadgets like GPS and other satellite systems – just turned off and wouldn't start again.

We were relatively safe in our school building – almost too safe. The administration decided that we should all be sent home for the day, but the system that automatically locks all the windows and doors during a lock-down was apparently tripped when the power surge went through the electrical system. Now, we were all locked in.

We were stuck inside for almost an hour

while parents gathered outside, waiting to pick up their kids, and the administrators and custodians scrambled to figure out how to get the doors unlocked. It would have been nice to hang out there with friends, but we were all kind of worried about our own families, since we couldn't get a hold of them by phone. All cell phone towers and landlines were down.

Most of the people living in town and the surrounding countryside gathered in the town square until sundown to get the latest news, since practically all electronic communication was useless. Only one guy with a ham radio was able to communicate with somebody outside of our town, but the signal was faint and the people operating the ham radios on the other end were just citizens like him trying to find out information.

By the time we were ready to go home that night, we hadn't even begun to realize how bad the situation was. It didn't look like the power was going to be restored anytime soon, but we still didn't know how widespread the problem was.

As several motorists ran out of gas along our highway and were forced to stay in our one small motel until the electricity could be restored to run the gas pumps, we learned from them that cities as far as 350 miles away were also affected. They all reported that they were desperately trying to get back home to check on loved ones, and that many of the cities and towns they had come from and traveled through were in much worse states than ours.

The motorists told of panic in the cities: people stuck in elevators and subway trains, thousands of car accidents as all of the stop-lights blinked off simultaneously, dozens of explosions at power plants and gas stations where power surges through the electronic pumps had ignited the tanks of fuel, small fires all over the cities, and people panicking everywhere. Part of me was glad to be here in the country, but another – a crazy, adven-turous side – kind of wished I was in a big city where all the excitement was.

When the sun set, an unusually brilliant orange sunset, there was a faint green glow in the northern sky that grew brighter as the sky got darker. The glow began to swirl and change colors like some kind of psychedelic gas-plasma ghost. As beautiful as it was, it was unnerving at the same time. Mr. Andre-sen explained that the phenomenon was called the Aurora Borealis and that it was a common sight in the northern latitudes. He added that the disturbance in the geomagnetic atmosphere from the solar superstorm made them visible much farther south. As we drove home that evening, we watched the colors dance in the sky and marveled at the wonder of nature.

That first night at home was strange, really, but a little fun. We had a gas generator, but Dad decided to not waste the gas to run it since he was convinced that the power would be back on soon. We had to keep the refrigerator shut to keep in the cool, so Mom made peanut butter sandwiches for dinner while Dad started a fire in the family room fireplace. It was still pretty warm outside, especially for November, but it got a little chilly at night. Plus it was fun to have a fire, something that we had been too busy to do for a while. Dad put a kettle of water on the fire and we made hot chocolate and roasted marshmallows, too. I wanted to roast hot dogs as well, but Dad reminded me that we couldn't open the fridge, so I had to make do with marshmallows and chips and whatever else I could find in the cupboards.

Mom lit candles in almost every room, and the house smelled like a mix of vanilla and cinnamon and oatmeal cookies, making me hungrier than ever. Then we all sat in the family room, around the fire, and talked. We hadn't done that in a long time either.

Alex was going crazy about not being able to call his girlfriend, Robin, and Calvin was going crazy about not being able to play his video games. I was happy to have the break in the normal routine. It felt like we stayed up late but really, we were in bed by 10:00 – early by my standards.

I woke up the next day at dawn. I had wanted to sleep in, but the combination of going to bed early, anticipation about what the day would bring, and waking up to a cold house got me out of bed right away. Dad and Mom were already up – with a fire going in the fireplace and the kettle of water whistling away – sipping at hot coffee and talking about what we needed to do today. They were in good moods – Mom because she had the day off from her job as a part-time accounts receivable clerk at the electric cooperative in town – "can't work at an electric company with no electricity," she joked – and Dad because the harvest was already in and he liked "roughing it."

Calvin was still asleep (lucky devil) and Alex had already gone to see his girlfriend, risking the last of his gas to fulfill his desire for love (or at least for making out). I was glad he was gone; things just seemed to be more pleasant when he wasn't around.

Mom and Dad decided we would do some chores around the house and farm, and then go into town after lunch if the electricity wasn't back on yet. It was kind of hard to do any cleaning around the house without electricity – we couldn't run the vacuum and we had to do the dishes by hand since the dishwasher wouldn't run. The worst part was that, without electricity, the pump on our well couldn't work, so we had to go outside to the old hand pump and manually pump the water into a bucket to carry inside. At first, the well water was all brown since the hand pump hadn't been used in ages, but after a while it cleared up. The toilet was acting weird, too, bubbling and gurgling, because of the water to the house being off.

Finally, after cleaning up the house the best we could, feeding the chickens and goats my Mom kept in a pen in the backyard, and eating our lunch of fresh eggs scrambled over the fire in the fireplace, we all climbed into Dad's big, extended-cab farm truck and drove the twelve miles into town.

Lots of people were gathered in the square again, and everyone seemed happy and excited, considering the circumstances. Old Man Riley, who owned the gas station, had somehow gotten ahold of a generator and was selling gas at an outrageous rate. He cited the fact that he now had to rent the generator and provide the fuel to run it. The stranded motorists were more than happy to pay the extra money, and most of them were already gone by the time we arrived in town. One poor guy, however, didn't have any cash or checks on him and without electricity, Old Man Riley couldn't run his credit card, so the townspeople took up a collection and bought him a tank of gas. He left declaring his undying gratitude for the town and promising to come back and repay each and every one of us who had helped him out. We assured him it wasn't necessary and wished him Godspeed (whatever that means) on his trip home to his family.

The highway, which ran through town, was eerily quiet most of the day, with just an occasional car or semi going by. Once, a hybrid car stopped for gas and its driver told us all that the power outage had spread at least as far as Denver, two states away, because that was where he had come from on his way home to Omaha. He said he was glad that he had a hybrid car, because there was no place to stop for gas or anything else in Kansas, and he had driven straight through. Otherwise, he probably would have run out of gas before now. Old Man Riley was glad to sell him some of his expensive gas, but refused to let him plug his car in to recharge for a while.

My friends and I had a great time wandering around the town, talking, tossing a football back and forth, and mildly harassing some girls. Around sundown, we were all getting a little cold and hungry, so we went back to the town square and found everyone gathering at Tipton's Diner, which now had a generator, food, and a somewhat warm place to eat. While our parents sat inside and talked, we kids sat out back on the picnic tables and messed around. Mr. Tipton had built a bonfire in the middle of the gravel parking lot and we all kept plenty warm.

Little by little, the bonfire died and the kids left to go home with their parents until I was left alone with Skylar Tipton, the owners' daughter. I hadn't talked much to Skylar for a long time because she had to work in the diner so much. That night, however, her parents had let her socialize with the rest of the kids, and it was nice to talk to her one-on-one for a change. I had known Skylar since we were little kids, but she seemed somehow different now – in a nice way.

When my parents were finally ready to go home, I didn't want to leave her. I tried to stall, but Skylar said she needed to go, too; her parents would be wanting her to help clean and close up the restaurant. I reluctantly went home with my parents, but it wasn't nearly as fun that time. I just wanted to call Skylar and talk to her more. That wasn't going to happen, of course, since the electricity still wasn't back on.

Mom said she had talked to her boss at the Electric Co-op, and he had told her that it could be a week before they had the opportunity to make the necessary repairs to get the electricity back on, and that was only if they could get their hands on parts soon enough. A serviceman had left in a company truck yesterday afternoon to see if he could get the parts in Kansas City, about ninety miles south of our town. No one had heard from him yet.

I went to bed even earlier that night. I felt unsettled and tossed and turned all night, thinking about the Skylar I thought I knew and the one I found out I didn't know at all.

Chapter 2

I woke up on the third day rather groggy from lack of sleep, and I blinked uncomprehendingly at the dark digital alarm clock for several seconds before I remembered that there was no electricity to keep track of the time. I knew it was later than normal, though, because the sun was already shining through my east-facing window. It was cold again, and I would have loved to stay there under the covers and think some more about this new, very attractive Skylar I talked to last night. I mean, she'd been there all along, all my life, really, but I guess I had not paid attention to how she was growing and changing all these years. Funny how something can be right in front of your eyes, but you don't really see it.

Anyway, as I was lying there in bed, the irresistible smell of bacon assaulted my nose like a line of C-dust (not that I've ever done it – I've just heard the class junkie, Irvine, talk about it. But with a name like Irvine, who wouldn't be driven to do drugs? I mean, my name's not great, but at least it sounds cool). I never could resist the smell of bacon, especially after two days of eating cold sandwiches and chips. I pulled on my jeans, a flannel shirt, and my favorite well-worn cowboy boots, and flew down the stairs, taking them three at a time.

Mom was in the kitchen, taking things out of the refrigerator, sorting some of them into piles on the counter and throwing others out the door to our three dogs, Ben, Shep, and Blue, who were lined up at the door, pushing and wiggling against each other to get into the best position to catch the next slightly spoiled treat. Every time she opened the door, I could hear the roar of the gas-powered generator hooked up to the circuit panel in our garage. Mom explained that Dad had decided to run the generator for a while to cool down the freezers – the one on top of the refrigerator and the big chest freezer in the garage filled with a side of beef and a whole butchered hog. The stuff in the refrigerator, however, was too warm to cool down again. Some could be cooked or eaten right away, but a lot of it had to be thrown out. The dogs were happy about it, though.

I don't remember ever enjoying a hot meal more – bacon, eggs, sausages, leftover chili and meatloaf, all made even tastier by cooking it over the logs in the fireplace. Dad told me to eat up because he had a lot of chores for me today. *Great*, I thought. I was hoping we'd have another carefree day of hanging around in town, maybe getting to talk to Skylar again.

"Where's Alex?" I asked Dad.

"He left before anybody was up this morning," he answered, looking slightly perturbed. "Probably had an itch to see that girl again." Dad usually didn't say much, but I could tell volumes from the tone of his voice and his particular phrasing of the sentence.

Maybe he was beginning to see the real Alex, the not-so-great Alex that I saw every day. I bowed my head down low over my plate to hide a little smile that I couldn't keep off my face.

After breakfast, Dad had me and Calvin take the chainsaw and the four-wheeler to the woods behind our house to gather firewood. I cut while Calvin loaded them into the little wagon behind the four-wheeler. When it was full, we drove it to the woodpile where Dad was splitting the logs into two, sometimes four, pieces to be used in the fireplace. Calvin and I started stacking the split logs neatly in a crisscross pattern onto the woodpile. We had learned long ago that wood stacking was an art and not one to be

18

done half-assed – not if you didn't want your ass tanned by Dad, that is.

Dad patiently explained every year when we cut firewood that, if you don't stack it right, it'll never dry out and be good to burn. He'd then follow up the words with a whack to the back of our heads or butts if we hadn't listened. He was like that – he'd explain things once, quietly and succinctly, and then you'd better have listened or he would remind you in a rather unpleasant way. He wasn't ever mean or angry about it; he just used it as a physical reminder to listen and follow directions.

Alex and I learned at a young age to listen to Dad, but Calvin was always more "recalcitrant", which was Mom's big word for stubborn and disobedient. This year, though, it seemed that Calvin had matured enough to accept Dad's authority without question; or maybe it was just the odd situation we found ourselves in that made him obey. Whichever the case, the woodpile got stacked without any problems.

All the hard work in the crisp autumn air made us all hungry again, so we went inside to find Mom frying up some rather gray-looking pork chops and lots of sliced potatoes and onions in a big cast-iron skillet she'd found in our camping gear in the garage. She was singing some old song from the seventies and doing a little dance, wiggling her rear end while she leaned over the fire. Mom was loving this!

She and Dad had always loved roughing it, taking us kids camping and spending quiet evenings at home around our fire pit in the backyard when we were growing up. We hadn't done either in the last couple of years because our lives had gotten so busy with sports and other school activities. I could tell Mom was happier than she had been in a long time. I could also tell that Dad was enjoying Mom's good mood, too, as he stood and watched her wiggle, a little smile dancing around the corners of his mouth.

"Are we going into town today?" I asked hopefully between mouthfuls of the surprisingly savory pork chops.

Dad pursed his lips while Mom answered cheerfully, "No, I think we need to go over to check on Granny and Gram and Papa."

Granny is Dad's widowed mother, and Gram and Papa are Mom's parents. They all lived in another town about thirty miles from our town in senior living apartments. Mom and Dad must have felt they were safe for the first couple of days without electricity, but now were starting to worry about how they were getting along. They were all in pretty good health – none of them needed oxygen or anything – but they were old and you never know how something like this would affect them. I started to ask if I could go into town instead, but a stern look from my father put that idea to rest right away.

We left a note for Alex on the kitchen table and took Mom's car since it got better gas mileage and had nearly a full tank. I won't say too much about our visit to the grandparents, except to say that they were having a grand old time, reminiscing about the old times with their "vintage homeys," as Calvin called their friends.

"Don't worry about us, dears," said Gram, "We used to live like this all the time, you know."

Even though they had had electricity in their day, living in the country back then meant spotty coverage with lots of outages. Most rural farm folk at the time just used electricity for lights and still relied on fireplaces and wood stoves for heat and cooking. They often still did laundry by hand and used clotheslines to dry them. Most had merely a radio for entertainment; even when

TVs were available, it was a long time before my grandparents got one. My Mom and Dad were in their early teens before their parents got TVs. Imagine no cartoons to watch when you were a kid, no shows to watch when you were bored after school. Well, we can imagine it now, because we're living it, but before PF Day I couldn't have.

On the way back home, I was able to talk Dad into going into town to "check on the electricity situation." If Dad didn't quite buy my fake intentions, he never let on. Maybe he wanted to "check on things" himself. On a normal day this time of year, he would have had breakfast at Tipton's Diner with his farmer friends and spent the morning talking about the weather, the harvest, grain futures, and whatever else farmers talk about in the off-season.

Don't get me wrong – farming is hard work. You work 18-hour days during the spring planting and the harvest in the fall, then you work hard all summer reinforcing levees along the river so the rain doesn't wash your topsoil away, working on your tractors and combine, leveling or terracing fields that are lying fallow in crop rotation, and hundreds of other things that always seem to take up a lot of time. Dad works hard from sunup to sundown for three-quarters of the year, so he and the other farmers deserve a break after harvest.

Anyway, Dad seemed as keen as I was to get to town to "check on things."

I was secretly pleased when Dad pulled into the gravel parking lot of Tipton's Diner. Calvin immediately jumped out of the car and ran off to find some friends, waving to Mom as he went to acknowledge her instruction to meet back there at sundown. Mom looked at me a little suspiciously as I led the way into the diner, something I'd never been known to do before.

I sat with Mom and Dad in a booth in the middle of the diner, while Dad immediately began talking with his cronies and Mom exchanged pleasantries with their wives. I was disappointed when Mrs. Tipton came over to the table instead of Skylar to ask us what we'd like to drink. The grill was off for now, she said, to save the gas in the generator for dinner service, but she could bring us water, tea, or sodas.

Dad ordered coffee, but Mrs. Tipton said it wasn't hot since the generator was off. Dad looked a little confused for a moment – he had never sat in the diner without a cup of hot coffee in front of him – before he quickly recovered and ordered iced tea instead. Mom and I ordered Pepsi and were a little surprised when it was brought back in cans instead of from the soda fountain.

"The fountain needs electricity," Mrs. Tipton explained, pouring the soda into glasses of half-melted ice for us.

I was sipping my Pepsi and trying to think of a nonchalant way to ask where Skylar was when I caught her looking at me from the kitchen. When she saw that I could see her, she motioned for me to come back there and I felt my face flush with excitement. I made a hasty excuse to my Mom and tried to look cool as I sauntered to the kitchen.

I'd never been in the kitchen before, despite having been to the diner probably a thousand times in my life. I was struck now by how dark it was in there, the only light coming from a small window on one wall and from the door leading into the dining area where large windows lined two walls. Skylar grinned at me, conspiratorially.

"I've been so bored today!" she whispered. "There's really nothing to do here with the power off and my parents won't let me run around with everyone. Maybe they'll let me talk to you outside like last night.

Wait here while I go ask."

I nodded enthusiastically and watched in admiration as she scurried off into the dining area to find her parents. I found I really liked her quirky style of thrown together clothes: turquoise sweater over an olive green flouncy skirt with navy blue leggings stuffed into worn brown cowboy boots. On anyone else, it would probably look careless, but it somehow suited Skylar with her slim figure and curly, light brown, shoulder-length hair. On her, it just looked adorable.

Like I said before, I'd known Skylar practically all my life, but I'd never really gotten to *know* her. Her parents were pretty protective of her, never letting her hang out with other kids or even to join any clubs or play sports. As far as I knew, she'd never gone out on a date, although that was not unusual for a fifteen-year-old. She spent most of her time after school and on weekends working with her parents at the diner. As an only child, they relied on her more and more to help out.

She came back to the kitchen with a broad smile on her beautiful face, grabbed her jacket with one hand and my hand with the other, and announced, "They said yes! Let's go!" Then, with a backwards glance at me as she pulled me out the door, she said, "We have to stay in the back, though. Mom said we could start a fire in the fire pit if we want to."

After we'd started the fire and pulled a couple of metal lawn chairs up close to it, I felt suddenly shy and awkward. Surprisingly, though, given that she'd never had a lot of interaction with kids her age, Skylar was not the least bit shy as she excitedly told me how great everything was going without electricity. For some reason, she was being allowed a little more freedom now – perhaps there wasn't as much work to do in the diner, or her parents were preoccupied with the loss of income that went along with the loss of power.

Whatever the reason, Skylar was ecstatic with the change and she declared that nothing would ever be the same from this day forward. Turns out, she was quite prophetic.

Skylar and I had the place to ourselves for a couple of hours until the sun started to set and townspeople began to show up for dinner. Mr. Tipton came out to start the generator and told Skylar she was needed in the kitchen. With a slight nod to me, he went back in and Skylar all of a sudden became shy. I couldn't understand the abrupt change in her until she surprised me with a quick kiss on my lips. Then she was gone. Just like that.

I'm embarrassed to admit that that was the first real kiss I'd had – the first one that mattered, anyway. Sure, I had been kissed by girls in elementary school, girls who had lost at truth or dare or who thought they had a crush on me, but never when I had wanted it. And oh, how I had wanted to kiss Skylar that night; only I had been too shy, too awkward, too – I don't know – too polite to initiate it. All I know for sure is that I was walking on clouds for the rest of the night.

We ate dinner in the diner, during which Skylar slipped me a huge chocolate chip cookie; "on the house," she whispered to me. The dinner was otherwise uneventful, although not as tasty as usual due to the lack of preparation and the limited menu, and we headed home in the darkness soon afterward. Alex didn't come home that night, which had my Mom in a near panic, but Dad convinced her he was probably just low on gas and was staying the night at Robin's house. Mom felt a little better until Calvin mischievously mentioned that they were probably busy making a baby right then, at which point he was sent to his room for the rest of the evening.

I said goodnight to Mom and Dad and went to my room, too, saying I was tired, which wasn't a lie, although I knew I'd never be able to sleep with the memory of that kiss and the image of Alex and Robin "making a baby" in my head.

All I can say is that it was a very, *very* long night.

Chapter 3

My family began to develop a pattern during the days following the power loss. We would get up around dawn and do chores in and out of the house, Mom would cook us something for breakfast (Dad had rigged up some grates in the fireplace to help her out), and for the first few days, we'd drive into town in the afternoon to check in on the latest news, if there was any. There usually wasn't any news, but it was nice to go into town and see friends anyway.

One day – I can't remember exactly which, but it was within the first couple of weeks when we still had gas to get to town – Bob Knadler, the serviceman from the electric company who had been sent to find parts to fix the blown transformers, finally made it back to town. The news he brought with him was grim.

Bob had made it to Kansas City, the biggest city to our south and the one most likely to have parts, but they had too many of their own emergencies to spare any equipment. Bob said he felt lucky to get out of there alive; apparently, if the power plants he had visited had been in the inner city – where thousands of desperate people were trying to leave by any means available – he might not have made it. Kansas City had had outages before, some lasting several days, but this situation was obviously not going to be fixed anytime soon and people were panicking.

There had been rioting and looting, made worse because the police were trying to conserve gasoline in their vehicles for major crises. Bob said that, right before he'd left Kansas City, the National Guard had come in and declared martial law. They believed that the Governor of Missouri would extend that martial law to the whole state soon. It appeared Kansas was going to do the same, as Kansas City, Kansas and Kansas City, Missouri are separated only by the Missouri River. Once again, I was happy to be living in the country; our whole family was –except for Alex.

Alex was driving us crazy. After his girlfriend's dad gave him just enough gasoline to get back home on the fourth morning, he begged and begged Mom and Dad to let him use their vehicles or to give him enough gas to get to Robin's house. Of course, they refused.

"You don't need to see her every day, Alex," and, "Let her come see you for a change," they told him. They also got him with, "You should have been more careful about conserving gas so you'd still have some," which just made him sulk even more. Everything out of his mouth was "Robin this" and "Robin that"; I was beginning to think he really was in love with her, but that didn't make hearing it constantly any better.

Eventually, they made a compromise: every other day, Mom and Dad would drop Alex by Robin's house on our way into town and pick him up on the way home; mostly, I think, just to shut him up for a while. He wasn't happy about the limited time with her, but it was better than nothing.

After about two weeks – two heavenly weeks of getting to see Skylar every day – our gasoline ran out. Well, not exactly. Dad had some gas in reserve in an underground tank that he used for his farm machinery. There wasn't much in the tank, however, because he had just finished the harvest and hadn't had it refilled before we lost power. He said we needed to make sure we had some in case of an emergency, and also some to run the generator as needed. He had to put a lock on it because he was pretty sure that Alex had become so desperate to see

Robin that he would steal some of the gas.

Surprisingly enough, I could now understand how Alex was feeling. After spending so much time with Skylar, my life at home now seemed dull and boring, like she had been the sun that brightened my day or a star that decorated my life at night.

Speaking of stars, I couldn't believe how bright the stars were. Mom said they'd always been that bright out here away from city lights, which was one of the thousands of reasons she and Dad had decided to live in the country, but I couldn't even remember looking at them, because my life had been so busy with school activities in the past few years.

Since we couldn't drive into town anymore, we had begun hanging out around the fire pit again in the evenings. It was chilly, but Mom would make us hot chocolate or, when that ran out, coffee, and we'd grab some long sticks and roast whatever meat was taken out of the deep freeze to thaw that day. We'd talk and look up at the sky; Dad would tell us which tiny, white dots were planets and which were stars. He mentioned how it was odd not seeing any planes or satellites in the sky anymore.

It was the first real inkling we had that

the power outage might be more widespread than just the Midwest. That was a scary thought – the whole world being affected by the solar flare – and no one wanted to say it out loud, but we were all thinking it. It made me wonder about the astronauts aboard the International Space Station. Would they have been hurt by the solar flare? And if they survived, how could they get in touch with NASA and the other space agencies, if everyone was without power around the world? They would be stranded out there, alone.

And the satellites; I could understand there being no planes in the air, but what about the satellites? I mean, even if we could get the electricity back on, without satellites there would be no television, no cell phones, no air travel.

I was beginning to think that Skylar wasn't just talking about *her* life never being the same again. Maybe none of ours would be. It was an even more unsettling thing to consider, so I tried to put it out of my mind and just focus on what was happening right then instead.

After about three weeks at home, a couple of men from the National Guard pulled up our drive in a jeep – the only vehicle we'd seen on the highway by our house in days – to tell us that the President had declared martial law for the entire United States and to ask if we needed any emergency supplies. After the initial shock of hearing that the whole country was impacted, we tried to ask them lots of questions, but they were in a hurry and didn't seem inclined to stick around to answer them.

The men did say, though, that it appeared it would be a long time before electricity was restored nationwide – however much time "a long time" was – and that we'd better start thinking of some way to survive the winter without it. They said that the priority was to restore power to the big cities first, where millions of people lived and didn't have access to wood and food like my family did. We understood – part of living in the country is always having backup plans when things don't go right. We were a little dazed, however, to realize that going to the city to stay in a hotel or get supplies probably wasn't going to be among those backup plans.

The thought of supplies got Mom thinking about the important things we needed to have on hand for the winter – important things like toilet paper. We could do without a lot of things, she said, or use something else instead of an item, like cloth hankies instead of Kleenex, but what were we to do without toilet paper?

Dad just chuckled and said, "We have a whole cornfield full of cobs out there, you know." Mom wasn't satisfied with that idea, however. After thinking about it all day, she came up with a solution. She hauled a couple of boxes of our old clothes up from the basement and began cutting the T-shirts and other soft clothes into four-inch squares. She said we could use those when the toilet paper ran out. I was grossed out thinking about having to wash all those stinky cloths, but Mom said she'd handle the laundry as long as my brothers and I pumped the water and hauled it in for her.

Dad, on the other hand, was thinking about big things. He decided we were going to need some form of transportation besides the gas-powered vehicles, and he had an idea of what that would be and where he could get it. He told me and my brothers to put on some "walkin' clothes" and we set out on foot to visit old Mr. Caruthers, who lived about eight miles away. Mom made us sandwiches and filled thermoses with coffee to take with us, as it would probably take at least a couple of hours to get there.

The walking was easy since we could walk on the highway without fear of being run over, and the day was nice – cool and sunny, so it wasn't too hot or too cold. We ate and drank as we walked and it was really kind of fun. Dad was more talkative than usual along the way, and he had lots of stories of when he was a kid and the crazy things he and his three brothers did. Even Alex was in a good mood, probably because he now realized that he could walk to Robin's house fairly easily after walking this far, as she lived only about six miles away from us.

Mr. Caruthers had a barn filled with old wagons and antique farm equipment, which he had collected over the years. Dad bartered a year's supply of corn and a pair of goats in exchange for a wagon and a couple of big geldings. He sure was glad that he had decided to store his grain in silos until the spring when prices would be higher; not only would we not starve, but he now had something to barter with. He also promised to come back with us boys to chop enough wood for the winter and do some handy work for Mr. and Mrs. Caruthers in exchange for a wagonload of hay and oats to feed the horses during the winter months.

The wagon we got was old, but in pretty good shape. Mr. Caruthers said it would probably need new boards on the sides soon, but that was easy to fix as we had some extra 1x8s at home. As Mr. Caruthers was showing us how to hitch up the horses, Dad spied a big, old pot-bellied stove in the corner of the barn and talked him into selling us that, too. It took all five of us to get that stove loaded into the wagon, but Dad seemed pleased with himself for getting it.

We rode home in style, Dad and I perched atop the bench of the wagon and Alex and Calvin in the back atop the bales of hay. Mom heard the dogs barking and she met us in the front yard with a big smile on her face, matched only by Dad's proud grin. The first problem immediately became apparent: where to keep the horses. We had a large barn, which housed the farm equipment, but there were no stalls inside for horses, and the pen that the goats and chickens were in was too small for horses to live in.

We had to crowd them in the pen temporarily while we set to work fixing up the barn and a larger outside area for them.

Luckily, Dad's grandfather, who had owned our farm before us, used to raise livestock, so we had three sides of an old post and wire fence already finished. We would just need to fix up what was there and add another side to complete a nice paddock for the horses.

Alex and Dad worked on clearing a space in the barn for the wagon and building a couple of stalls while Calvin and I took the four-wheeler and wagon into the woods to find trees to cut for fence posts. Dad had told us to look for cedars about five inches in diameter and seven or eight feet tall. We had to drive all over our sixty acres of woods to find enough cedars that fit the bill, but by the end of the day, we had cut and carried back nearly two dozen of them.

The next day, we got to work setting the fence posts. Even with a tractor-powered auger, it was hard work, especially when we had to replace some of the old posts by first digging them up. There was a large spool of 12-gauge wire in the loft of the barn, which we were able to wrangle down between the four of us.

We spent the entire third day stringing that wire between the posts of the new side of the fence and replacing downed wire along the old sides. The only thing left to do on the fourth day was to build and attach a gate to the pasture.

That was the hardest four days of work we boys had ever had to do, but we all felt such a sense of accomplishment when we were finally able to let the horses loose in their new paddock. We stood and leaned against the gate just like in an old Western movie and watched the horses frolic around. Mom came out to watch them, too, and said, "There's just something about watching horses that makes you feel really alive."

I had never just stood and watched horses before, even though several of my friends were avid horse lovers and they'd dragged me along to horse shows and rodeos with them. I was usually people-watching at those events and thought the horses were just big, sweaty, smelly creatures, but now, as I stood watching our horses stretch out their legs, running and jumping all over the paddock, I finally understood what my friends saw in them. It was as if God had rolled beauty and grace and power all up into one big package. They moved so effortlessly, but you could feel their raw strength and power through the ground as they galloped close by the gate.

At that moment, I wanted more than anything in the world to have Skylar here, to let her experience what I was feeling, to share that sense of wonder and joy with her.

Chapter 4

It was around a month or so after PF Day (although we weren't calling it that yet) that Mom decided we needed to continue our schoolwork at home. She brought out all of the reading material in the house and asked us what textbooks we had at home. I had only brought home Geometry and World History. Calvin didn't bring anything home; he always got his homework done at school. Like I said, he's real smart.

Alex protested that since he was a junior and had already completed all of his core requirements, he shouldn't have to do school, so Mom told him to help Dad with the farm for the rest of his junior year credits. "It'll be like going to a technical school," she said. That didn't make Alex too happy, but he knew better than to push his luck.

Later, I overheard Mom talking to Dad about the need to go into town to pick up our textbooks from the school and get supplies. Dad didn't think there'd be anything left at the grocery store or farm supply, but he was willing to hitch up the wagon to go see. I was ecstatic, of course. The chance to see Skylar again was a gift better than anything I could have thought of. It seemed like

Christmas morning to me; I was that excited.

I eagerly volunteered to help Dad get the horses and wagon ready, but Mom said, "No, that's Alex's assignment." Alex frowned and grumbled a little, but he could hardly argue, since it was kind of *his* idea to not do regular schoolwork.

We were on the road before nine in the morning. We probably resembled a pioneer family altogether in the wagon with the horses plodding along.

Dad and Alex had loaded several big, plastic buckets with the three grains he had harvested a couple of months ago – corn, soybeans, and wheat – to trade for things we needed. Mom packed us a lunch in Great Grandma's old wicker picnic basket, and we ate on the way. It was fun; we laughed and told jokes and stories, and then, after we ate, Calvin and Alex laid down in the back of the wagon for a little catnap.

I was too excited to sleep, so I just day-dreamed while Mom and Dad chatted about what they needed to try to get in town. On the way, we stopped by several neighbors' houses to see if they needed anything, but all had pretty much taken care of things on their own. You see, farmers are an independent, self-reliant type of people, for the most part.

It took us about four hours to get to town, so we knew we couldn't stay very long if we wanted to get home before dark. It was going to be a full moon, though, so we knew we could probably travel in the dark if we needed to. Dad dropped Mom, Calvin, and me off at the school while he and Alex went to the square to find supplies.

We found that the school was locked up tight, so we walked over to the superintendent's house down the street. When Mom explained why she wanted in the school, the superintendent was more than happy to let us in. After we had gathered our textbooks and some reading books from the library, we walked to the town square to meet Dad and Alex.

I was dying to see Skylar, so after stowing my books in the wagon, I asked if I could walk around on my own. Mom said that I could as long as I came back to the square in one hour. I took off at a run in the direction of the diner, which I could already tell was closed. Skylar and her parents lived down the block behind the diner, so I turned the corner at the restaurant and headed their way.

When I knocked on their door and no one answered, I was dismayed and disappointed. Where could they have gone? It wasn't as if they could just get in their car and go to the city or something. They had to be around town somewhere, maybe visiting a neighbor. I couldn't just go door-to-door, asking everyone if they knew where Skylar was, and so I just started walking around town, up and down streets with my hands in my pockets and my hat pulled down over my ears against the December chill.

After about ten minutes – ten agonizing minutes of knowing that my possible time with Skylar was ticking away by the second – I spotted her with a group of kids hanging out in front of Caleb Stein's house. Try as I might, I couldn't keep the huge grin off my face as I jogged over to them.

"Bracken!" several of the girls squealed together.

"Hey, Fern, where've you been?" Caleb asked jokingly when I reached them. Oh, how I wish I'd never let slip what my name really means. But now, I was just happy to be so readily welcomed, that I couldn't care less what they called me. You see, I've never been the real popular type. I'm more the quiet, studious nerd type, but in a small town, where everyone has grown up to-gether, I was never bullied or ostracized, just not the most sought-after friend either. But today, it seemed like I was the one everyone was excited to see. It was probably because they hadn't seen me in such a long time – me being isolated out on the farm and all. Even Irvine, the stoner, spoke to me. He looked pale and haggard, his eyes like a couple of dull marbles set in a skull's empty sockets.

"Hey," was all he said, but that was more than he usually said to me.

"What's been going on in town?" I asked, trying to surreptitiously maneuver myself over to Skylar's side. To my delight and embarrassment, she grabbed my hand and pulled me close, looking up at me with a big smile on her beautiful face. It was really hard to concentrate on what any of my friends were saying with her being so close. Even though I was happy to see my friends, all I really wanted was to be alone with Skylar.

The kids talked of life in town now – boring, but also sort of cool facing so many new challenges every day. Except that several of the older and sicker people in and around town had died despite the townspeople's efforts to pull together and help everyone out.

One boy, Bob Newton, uncharacteristically had tears in his eyes as he told about he and his family trying to save his grandma, who died while gasping for air after her oxygen tank had run out. Suddenly, I was worried about my grandparents. I made a mental note to bring them up to my parents when I got back to the wagon, just in case.

I looked at my watch and noticed with dismay that I had only twenty minutes left before I had to get back. As if reading my thoughts, Skylar said to the group, "I'd better be getting home. My parents will worry if I'm not home before dark." Her hand squeezed mine. "Brack, will you walk me home?"

The way she said it told everyone that she wanted to be alone with me, and I was swept away by feelings of pride, acceptance, happiness, and something else – love? I was pleased that she had made up a nickname for me, something only she called me. I decided to start calling her Sky, which seemed particularly suitable to me since she reminded me of heavenly things. We said goodbye to everyone and Skylar gave each of the girls hugs while the guys patted me on the back and said, "Come back soon, man," and other things like that, making me feel very important and welcome. So this must be how it feels to be popular. I could get used to this. Having a girlfriend *and* being accepted by the cool guys – nice!

Skylar and I walked very slowly back to her house and stopped on the corner a few houses down the street under a huge oak tree. It was starting to get really cold with the sun going down, so Skylar cuddled up close to me and I put my arms around her. Then, we started kissing. I won't go into too much detail, but let me just say that "heavenly" does not even begin to describe it. For the first time in my life, I didn't care that I'd be late or that I might get in trouble. This was definitely worth any amount of punishment I could receive.

After a while, though, Skylar pulled away and said, with a sad little frown on her face – which looked adorable, by the way – that she had to get home and that I'd better be going, too, so I wouldn't get into trouble. It touched me that she was worried about me.

"When will you be able to come back to town?" she asked, hopefully.

"Maybe I can talk my parents into letting me take one of the horses and ride back here," I answered with sudden inspiration.

"I'm not too good at riding yet, but I'm learning."

"Oh, please do!" she exclaimed. "I want to learn to ride, too. Jenny Garten said she'd teach me. Maybe we could go riding together sometime."

"That'd be great!" I grinned. "Maybe I can come back in a couple of days."

At that, Skylar kissed me deeply and reluctantly drew away to walk home. I stood and watched her until she stepped through her front doorway, stopping halfway to blow me a kiss and wave goodbye. I waved back, but she was already in the house. I wasn't sure if her parents had returned yet or not, but thinking of parents, I looked at my watch and realized I was already ten minutes late getting back to the wagon, so I took off at a run to the town square, several blocks away.

When I arrived, my Mom merely gave me a perturbed look before she softened, asking if I'd had a good time seeing my friends. The way she said it made me feel like she knew exactly whom I'd been with and what we'd been doing. But she seemed happy about it, pleased in a way, and I felt myself blush even though I was glad that Mom wasn't upset about the situation.

Alex was helping Dad finish up loading some buckets and sacks of stuff into the wagon, but Calvin didn't get back until ten minutes later. Mom admonished him sternly, but didn't say anything about a punishment. After all, what could she do: ground us, take away our video game time, find even more chores than what we were already doing?

This new life had its advantages, even if I couldn't see Skylar as much as I wanted. But if it hadn't been for PF Day, Skylar and I probably would never have gotten together. Life is funny that way: sometimes the worst catastrophes can result in the best things.

As we bumped along home in the wagon, I told Mom and Dad about the senior citizen deaths and my concerns about my grandparents. They grimly answered that they'd heard about them, too, and that they had already decided to make a trip to get them and bring them to our house.

Mom said we would have to think about where to put them, and that probably two of us boys would have to give up our rooms, but that was all right with me. Dad said that maybe we could fix up the basement for them and put that pot-bellied stove down there for warmth this winter. There was a toilet and a sink down there that would have to be enclosed with walls, but no tub for bathing. Not that we were able to have a full bath anyway. We were only able to heat a bucket-full of water and use a washcloth to wash ourselves.

Mom was concerned about them having to climb up the stairs, but Dad pointed out that our rooms were upstairs and that the only alternative would be to make the living and dining rooms into rooms for them, effectively cutting off our access to the fireplace, which we needed for heat and cooking. He said if they were downstairs, we could take anything they needed down to them and maybe he could even fashion them some kind of lift in the future. At any rate, it was decided to fix up the basement during the next couple of days before we would bring them home.

I asked Dad what supplies they were able to get in town, and Alex answered enthusiastically, which was uncharacteristic of him, that the town had set up a makeshift trading center in the square where people could bring things they didn't need to trade for what they did. Dad and Alex were able to trade our grain for a couple of big cans of shortening, and restaurant-sized cans of green beans and coffee from Tipton's Diner (so that was where Skylar's parents had been), half a dozen old oil lanterns from Mr. Caruthers, and a box full of scented beeswax candles from Candee Smith, who owned Candee's Candles.

I asked what we would use for fuel in the oil lamps and Dad said we might be able to use the shortening. I was sure glad we got some things to light our evenings, as it had become too cold to sit outside, and darkness fell so early now. It was hard to all sit around the fireplace every night, trying to get close enough to read. I just wanted some time to myself every once in a while.

Mom was excited that she was able to get some plants from Mrs. Littleton's Greenhouse. She got some medicinal herbs like lemon balm, feverfew, and licorice root, along with edibles: strawberries, cherry tomatoes, and seeds for planting in the spring. She also got a few books on medicinal herbs and their uses. She couldn't wait to get home and read up on the plants and herbs that could be found in our own yard, like dandelion, marigold and Echinacea, and how to harvest them for medicinal use.

Sometimes I think Mom is what Granny calls an "old soul," someone who seems to have lived a past life in the old days and vaguely remembers some of it. Mom certainly acts like this is the kind of life she's used to and enjoys the most. I'm beginning to think maybe I am a little bit of an old soul, too, and Dad is definitely one.

When we got home that night, it was nice to light a candle and take it to my room, snuggle under my quilt that Gram made me for Christmas when I was seven, and read a book I had borrowed from the school library. It helped, somewhat, to take my mind off Skylar, but still, my mind kept wandering to her and that heavenly make-out session. I was tired, though, and it wasn't long before I fell asleep.

The next day, I was up with the sun and, as usual, so were Mom and Dad. Alex and Calvin both came downstairs not long after me, so we all ate a nice breakfast of bacon, eggs, and coffee as a family.

Dad had our day already planned out for us, so while Mom fed the animals, collected eggs from our chickens, and looked for plants in the yard to harvest for medicinal uses, Dad started us boys on building partitions in the basement for enclosing the bathroom and making two bedrooms for our grandparents, leaving the largest part of the basement open for a common area. We had some plywood and other lumber on hand to build with, but at one point we had to tear out some old walls in the barn to finish up the rooms. It looked a little rough when we were done, but Dad reassured me that it would all look good once the walls were painted.

He was right, as usual. We painted everything with a couple of gallons of leftover paint that we mixed together to make a light bluish shade that covered the space. Mom came down when the basement was complete and declared it "very homey, indeed", which was Mom's way of saying "nice job."

Mom took several area rugs from upstairs and in storage – we had all hardwood floors upstairs covered in area rugs – to cover the cement floor of the basement. The rugs were big enough to cushion most of the open space and make the floor a little warmer for my grandparents.

She also brought down any extra pieces of furniture we didn't use often, and even her favorite easy chair. Dad donated his favorite chair, as well, and with the loveseat from the family room and our small dining table, the place looked pretty good. I offered my bed for them, but Mom said that they would bring their beds with them from the assisted living center if they could fit them in the wagon.

The next day, Dad had us help install the pot-bellied stove. It took all four men in our house, and even some help from Mom, to get it down the stairs from the cellar door on the outside of the house. We installed it under a window halfway down the outside wall of the open area so it faced the doors to the bedrooms. We had to run the flue out through the window and fix a board around it to fill up the hole. Then, we cleared a place on the wall beside the steps to the cellar door to stack firewood, which we did next.

We started the stove to test it out and, after it burned for about an hour, it got so hot down there that Dad decided to divert some of the heat to the house's heating ducts to send it upstairs to heat our own bedrooms. He told Mom to close off the heating vents in the first floor rooms and that night, for the first time since the cold weather set in, our bedrooms weren't freezing cold.

Dad placed a thermometer in each of our rooms and found that they were 60°, while the basement was a toasty 70°. He was so pleased with the result that he walked around rubbing his hands together like over a fire and saying it felt like summer.

It was sure nice sleeping that night, what with a candle to read by before falling to sleep and then sleeping in a heated room. The next morning, I wasn't nearly so eager to hop out of bed.

Chapter 5

Mom and Dad left a couple of days later at dawn to get our grandparents. They left us boys at home to save space in the wagon for any cargo to be brought back. They said they'd probably have to stay away overnight, because it would take about seven hours to get there and it would be too dark and too cold to travel back at night.

Mom told us to stay at home but, of course, Alex didn't listen. He left on foot for Robin's house as soon as they were out of sight. I briefly considered walking to town to see Skylar, but I didn't have the nerve to walk that far on my own and it didn't feel right to disobey Mom.

Dad had left us instructions to do some repair work around the farm, like fixing some loose boards on the chicken coop and mending a spot in the goat pen where they had repeatedly climbed on the fence and stretched the wires. I was a little pissed off that Alex wasn't going to be around to help us, but Calvin stepped up and did more than his part with enthusiasm I didn't know he had; together, we had everything done by late morning.

We were in the house, eating lunch when we heard the sound of hooves on our gravel driveway out front. Calvin and I look at each other, surprised and concerned that Mom and Dad were coming back so soon. We ran outside to find, to my astonishment and great excitement, Skylar and Jenny Garten on a pair of horses in our yard.

"Hey, Brack," Skylar said. There was that nickname again. "Hi, Calvin."

I was struck speechless for a few seconds, during which time Calvin sidled up to Jenny's horse and started stroking its neck.

"Uh, hi, Sky," I stammered. I realized that it sounded a little dumb, the way it rhymed and all, but Skylar seemed to like it. She smiled and slid off her horse to put her arms around me and give me a quick kiss.

Then she looked a little worried and said, "Your parents can't see us, can they?"

"Nah, they're not home, but even if they were, I don't think they'd care," I assured her. She looked relieved, but her brow was still furrowed in confusion. I'm sure she was thinking that her parents would kill her if they saw her kissing a boy.

Jenny was talking to Calvin, and then said a little louder to include me, "You guys want to go for a ride with us?"

"Sure!" Calvin and I answered simultaneously, which made all of us laugh.

"Jinx," we said at the same time again, and that made us all laugh a little harder. I know we looked a little giddy, but hell, we hadn't seen anybody besides our immediate family in several days, and they were pretty girls besides. Even Calvin, who up to now hadn't shown much interest in girls, seemed to be showing off for them.

We jumped up behind the girls and rode all over the place, stopping now and then to run into the house to grab food or to let the horses rest.

Surprisingly, Skylar was quite a good rider. She explained that after I had left town a few days ago, she had asked Jenny to give her riding lessons so she could ride out to visit me. I was both impressed and flattered that she would go to so much trouble just to see me. It was so exciting to be sitting behind her on that horse with my arms around her waist and her silky hair blowing in my face. I was becoming quite the horse lover for more reasons than one.

I asked Skylar how she had gotten her parents to consent to her traveling so far to see me. She gave me an ornery little smile over her shoulder and said, "Oh, they don't know. They think I'm staying over at Jenny's."

Staying over at Jenny's – that phrase stuck in my mind. So, she wasn't expected home and my parents weren't coming home that night... If only we could figure out a way for Jenny to be able to stay.

When I shyly brought up my idea to the girls, Jenny said no way. Skylar seemed a little hesitant, too, and I suddenly realized where their thoughts were going. Flushed, I quickly assured them that they could sleep in my parents' bed and that we could stay up late sitting around the fireplace and talking.

Skylar was game after that and Jenny seemed more at ease with it, but she was still convinced that her parents would freak if she didn't come home that night. I reluctantly gave up on the idea.

The girls had to leave at around three in the afternoon in order to be home by nightfall, but before they left, Skylar lingered in my arms making out with me. Calvin and Jenny rode a little ways away and talked embarrassedly while we kissed. I know I probably should have been a little embarrassed myself, making out in front of my little brother, but at the time all I could think of was how great it felt and how I didn't want it to end.

But it did end, and I stood and watched them ride away until the curve of the highway prevented it. It made me think of those classic Westerns where the woman watches her man ride away into the sunset; except that I was watching my girl ride away, and it wasn't sunset yet.

Alex didn't come home that night. Calvin and I were convinced that he was taking the opportunity to sleep with Robin again. Robin lived alone on a farm with her dad, Joe. Her mom had died when she was a toddler, and her dad had never remarried or had any other children. Alex had once mentioned to Calvin and me how easy it was to sneak around behind her dad's back and that they could do almost anything they wanted to. He had put special emphasis on the word *anything* and winked in a way that left no doubt in our minds what he was implying.

Calvin and I spent a boring evening playing Monopoly by candlelight and talked about the girls' visit earlier in the day. Calvin seemed to have a little crush on Jenny, which I thought was funny, considering she had at least two years on him. I didn't think he'd have a chance with her, since he was just a kid and she was in high school. I didn't tell him that, though. It was the first time he'd expressed any interest in a girl in that way and I didn't want to discourage him.

The next day, Calvin and I took extra time to clean up the house and yard to make everything nice for when our family came home. They arrived around two o'clock in the afternoon, and what a sight they made as they came plodding up the road in the wagon. They looked just like those old re-runs of the *Beverly Hillbillies* that we used to watch when nothing else was on, with Dad and the grandmas on the bench seat and Mom and Papa perched on top of the mattresses in the back of the wagon. Not to mention the mounds of *stuff* piled all around them. Calvin and I busted out laughing at the sight, and we ran down the highway to greet them.

When we had begun to unload everything, Dad asked where Alex was. Calvin and I looked at each other, neither one of us wanting to break the news to them. After a few seconds, I answered, "He walked over to Robin's house yesterday and…" I didn't bother to finish.

All Dad said was "Damn!" under his breath. Mom just shook her head and turned back to unloading the stuff.

Granny, Gram, and Papa were tired from the journey, so Mom insisted they lie down on our beds while we fixed up their rooms downstairs. Mom was unusually quiet about Alex's disappearance. I think she was disappointed that he had disobeyed her and had given no thought to how much his absence would make her worry. Maybe she was kind of upset about him getting old enough to leave home soon, too. It made me sad to think of her being upset, so I made sure to give her extra hugs and help her with whatever she was doing the rest of the afternoon. It seemed to cheer her up some.

My grandparents came downstairs later and were very pleased with what we had done for them in the basement. They all decided that they would be very comfortable here and began making themselves right at home while Mom fixed us all some dinner. We all ate downstairs at the dining table and had a good time catching up on things that had happened since we had last seen each other.

At one point, Granny told us, with tears in her eyes, how many of the residents of the assisted living apartments where they had been living had died or were on the verge of dying without the medicines they needed to stay alive. It made me sad to think of all the kids who had lost their grandparents and made me very grateful that my own grandparents were in good health.

That evening, after the sun had set and the stars were twinkling brightly in the sky, Alex came home. He brought Robin with him. Her eyes were all puffy and red, and her nose was shiny. Alex was grim and I could tell right away that something was very wrong. Mom and Dad must have known, too, because they didn't even scold him; they just asked, "What happened?" to which Robin began crying again. She hid her face in Alex's shoulder.

"Robin's dad was hurt real bad yesterday." I could tell Alex was trying not to cry, too. "A bull kicked him in the belly. He was bleeding really bad when I got there, and Robin didn't know what to do, so I ran as fast as I could to the Jenkins' place and brought them back to help, but it was too late." Alex started choking up. He barely got the next words out. "He died last night, and we buried him this morning."

Mom swept in and put her arms around the both of them, murmuring over and over, "Oh, I'm so sorry," between sobs.

I was stunned into silence. I had never experienced a death so close to my family before. I mean, my grandpa on my Dad's side had died when I was little, but I didn't remember him at all, and a kid named Sid Eldon from the next town over had wrecked his car and died, but he was a lot older than me and I hadn't really known him.

But Robin's dad, Joe McKnight, was part of our small community; I saw him often and heard his name even more. He was a friend of Dad's and he was healthy and strong. Suddenly, life without power and gas-powered vehicles didn't seem so cool, after all. I wasn't sure how to act or how to make Alex and Robin feel better. I glanced at Dad to see how it was affecting him, but he had turned away and was stoking the fire. It didn't need stoking.

Mom made Robin a strong cup of tea out of some of the herbs she had been growing and laid her down in Alex's bed. Alex lay next to her and held her in his arms until she went to sleep, and then came downstairs to talk to Mom and Dad.

"She can stay here, can't she?" he asked pitifully. "I mean live here with us? She doesn't have anyone else."

"Well, of course she can stay," Mom answered soothingly, putting her arm around Alex. "You can move into one of your brothers' rooms and she can stay in yours. Did you bring her any clothes or anything?"

"No, she just wanted to get away from there as soon as we could. She's a wreck."

"Poor thing. What a horrible thing to have to see." Mom shook her head and brushed away new tears forming in her eyes.

"It was awful, Mom. All that blood. I didn't want to leave her there alone with him, but I had to try to get help." Alex laid his head on Mom's shoulder just like a little kid. "I'm sorry I disobeyed you yesterday, Mom, but I'm glad I went. For Robin's sake."

"Yes, don't worry about it, sweetie," Mom soothed. "It'll be alright." They sat like that for a long time until Alex gave in to exhaustion and decided to go to bed.

I felt really sorry for Alex for the first time in a long time. Of course, I felt even sorrier for Robin, but I was surprised at the depth of emotion I felt for my big brother. I felt kind of protective of him, so I told him to go sleep in my bed and that I'd find someplace else to sleep. He looked at me tenderly with tears in his eyes and said, "Thanks, Buddy." Then, he reached out and gave my shoulder a little squeeze before slowly, painfully, climbing the stairs to my room.

The rest of us sat in the family room around the fire, holding each other real close and not talking much. Gram and Papa were the first to go to bed, then Granny left, too, but Mom, Dad, Calvin and I sat for a long time just holding each other. For the first time in over a month, I didn't think of Skylar.

Chapter 6

For the next couple of weeks, Robin was just a shell of her former happy-go-lucky self. She cried at the drop of a hat and barely ate anything for days. That was understandable, of course. She had just lost the only parent she had ever known and did not even have any other relatives to live with. She was forced to live with her boyfriend's family and even though we were all very friendly and tried to be comforting to her, there is just no replacing your own family at a time like that.

The change in Alex, however, was much more profound – at least it seemed that way to me, because even though he hadn't lost a family member, it was like it had been a life-changing event for him. Gone was the self-centered, self-righteous, self-important teenager. In his place was a caring, responsible, and even humble adult.

Alex didn't wait to be told to do something anymore; if he saw something that needed to be done, he did it without hesitation or complaint. He was very helpful to Mom, carrying stuff up and down the stairs for her, helping her with the laundry, which was quite a chore by hand, and even pitching in to clean the house. He worked alongside Dad like he was a partner on the farm, something which, I'm sure, pleased Dad immensely.

He was especially tender and comforting to Robin, holding her when she cried, bringing her hot tea and food to her room when she didn't feel like coming downstairs. And, most baffling of all, he was nice toward Calvin and me.

It was like Mom always joked when we behaved a little too well for some reason: "What alien replaced Alex with you and where did he take the real one?"

We were all pleased with the change, although we didn't know how long it would last. I kept waiting for the other shoe to drop, for Alex to box my ears or snatch some food out of my hands like he used to. But for now, we were happy with him.

A couple of weeks after Robin's dad died, a big army Hummer stopped by the house. We heard it coming like a mile away since there was never any traffic anymore. We were all lined up out front when it drove up. A couple of National Guardsmen stepped out and asked if we needed any medical or emergency supplies. Mom said we could use some antibiotics, painkillers and such to have on hand in case of an emergency, so one of the Guardsmen got a small box from the back of the Hummer and gave it to Mom. Robin was apparently thinking how she wished they'd have come two weeks ago, when her dad desperately needed the painkillers, because she started to cry again and ran into the house.

Dad asked if there was any news from the rest of the country and the Guardsmen told us that it looked grim for the entire civilized world. Some power had been restored to parts of a few major cities, but it wasn't enough to stop thousands of deaths from starvation, dehydration, lack of emergency medical care, and exposure to cold.

They mentioned that while we were enjoying a relatively mild December so far, there had been a severe cold snap and a blizzard in the Northeast that was causing all kinds of misery. One of the biggest problems, they said, was getting fresh water into the cities. After the water stored in the water towers ran out, there wasn't any easy way to get water to citizens packed into the metropolitan areas.

A lot of people were pretty resourceful, collecting rainwater and snow in any kind of container possible on top of the buildings, but many places did not get enough precipitation to provide water for everyone. There wasn't enough gasoline left for tankers to bring water into every city every day. It made me wonder what our little town was doing to get water, and I told myself to remember to ask Skylar the next time I saw her.

Heat was a problem, too, since there were few trees to burn in the cities, and not very many houses had wood-burning fireplaces anyway. The Guardsmen said that many people were burning furniture, books, clothing, and even parts of their houses in their ovens and bathtubs. This caused a lot of people to collapse from smoke inhalation, and a lot of buildings to catch on fire, fires which then spread from house to house or building to building, without water to put them out.

Most communities set up shelters inside schools and churches and other community buildings where they put together safer methods of providing heat, though it wasn't nearly enough to keep everyone warm. These shelters were the first places that power was restored to, when it was available, and became havens for many people living in the cities.

Food had also become scarce. At first, grocery stores had been reluctant to give out provisions, but after the first week, those that wouldn't share were looted anyway, until there wasn't any food left. And, of course, no way to get any more, as every community was facing the same shortages and could not share. The army had taken over the big grain silos countrywide and was rationing out grain to as many as possible. The Guardsmen thought that the army would soon start taking livestock from farmers to help feed people, even though that would financially ruin those farmers in the process.

They also warned us of roving gangs of looters wandering the countryside, taking whatever they could from everyone. Desperate times called for desperate measures, they said. They told us to arm ourselves and to be sure to save bullets, if we had any, in case we had to defend our property and, possibly, our lives.

Luckily, we had some rifles and shotguns for deer hunting, although we had totally forgotten about hunting season that November. It sounded like it was a good thing we had forgotten, so we still had the stash of bullets Dad had bought for the season barely a week before PF Day. When our freezer full of beef and pork ran out we would have to hunt with our compound bows, if the power was still off at that time.

After the Guardsmen had left to visit other farms along the highway, Dad got to thinking about old Mr. and Mrs. Caruthers. He said it would be best to make a point of checking on them once a week or so, to make sure they were safe and well supplied. We made plans to take the wagon with several sacks of grain to their house the next day and to spend the day fixing up their place for winter. Alex was reluctant to leave Robin, but she said it was time that she stopped being such a baby and started helping out around the house, and that Alex should go help the Caruthers's. Of course, we all assured her that she was not being a baby and Mom gave her a big hug, saying, "Welcome back, sweetheart." Robin seemed to really enjoy having a mother figure and she smiled for the first time since she had come to our house.

By the time Dad, Alex, Calvin and I had loaded up the wagon and were ready to set out to the Caruthers's house the next day, Mom and Robin had made us thermoses of coffee and lunches to eat on the way. Gram and Granny also had made a cake from scratch and baked it in the coals of the fire in an old Dutch oven that we had occasionally used for camping. They told us it was a gift for Mr. and Mrs. Caruthers, and when we started to protest good-naturedly, they laughed and said they had made us one, too; it was already stowed in our picnic basket. I hadn't had cake for almost two months, and my mouth started watering immediately at the promise of one.

On the way, we all decided to eat the cake first – who knew when we would ever get something so wonderful again, we reasoned. It was probably the most delicious cake I'd ever eaten, although there is a good possibility that it was just because of the rarity of cake these days. Between the four of us guys, we devoured the entire thing and, for the first time in a couple of weeks, we were content.

We found Mr. and Mrs. Caruthers doing fairly well, although Mrs. Caruthers complained that her arthritis was giving her a lot of trouble since she was out of her medicine. I told her that I would ask Mom if she knew of any herbal remedies that would be of some help, and Mrs. Caruthers said, with tears in her eyes, "God bless you, dear."

With her mind a bit more at ease, she asked us what we were planning to do for Christmas. I was surprised by the question, because I hadn't even remembered that the holidays were coming up. Christmas used to be my favorite time of the year, but now it seemed so superficial and artificial.

When I shrugged my shoulders, Mrs. Caruthers said, "If I know your Mom, she'll have something special planned."

That got me to thinking. For the rest of the day, while I worked on chopping wood, fixing loose shingles on their roof, and setting bales of straw around their foundation to help insulate the house for winter, I thought about what I could make or do for each person in my family for Christmas. For the first time in my life, I started thinking – really thinking – about Christmas as a time of giving to others instead of a time to get the latest toys and gadgets. As ideas for gifts started to form in my brain, I began to get excited about the things I could do to make the people I love happy. I decided not to say anything to anybody about Christmas so I could surprise them with my gifts.

When we got home that evening, satisfied with our hard work and the chance to help out our neighbors, Mom and Robin, with the help of my grandparents, had already decorated the house for Christmas. It was as if they had somehow overheard me and Mrs. Caruthers talking earlier. Mrs. Caruthers had been right – there was no way Mom would forget Christmas.

Even though there were no lights on the tree, it looked beautiful anyway, covered with all of our old ornaments to remind us of our normal life. Mom said Christmas was in just four days and she had been planning, for some time, to surprise us with the decorations. I had kind of lost track of the time. I mean, I knew it was December, but I hadn't looked at a calendar in weeks. There was really no need to: no school or work to have to go to, no church services to go to on Sunday, etc. The fact that the year was practically over with had caught me off guard.

I wondered if our church would plan something for Christmas Eve, as they always had in the past. When I asked Mom, she said we'd just go there on Christmas Eve and say a prayer, whether anyone else was there or not.

Since our church was in the country instead of the town, it had remained closed for the two months since PF Day, but Mom was pretty sure people would gather there if they could, even without electricity. After all, she said, it was a candlelight service, not an electric light service.

The next day, after my regular chores were done and I had finished the schoolwork that Mom had assigned me, I got to work on the Christmas gifts I had planned for everyone. It was hard to keep everything a secret, and Calvin ended up catching me working on a gift for Mom in the barn. He begged me to let him help and wouldn't let up until I said he could. We worked together on presents for everyone in our family except each other and, though I had originally wanted to do the job all on my own, I had to admit that we were able to make much better gifts together than I could have by myself. We worked for the next three days and, in the end, we were pretty satisfied with the results.

We arranged with our grandparents to keep Mom busy in the basement while we carried her present into the utility room and covered it with a blanket and a sign to not open it until Christmas. The other gifts were easier to wrap in old newspapers tied with ribbon and would be placed under the tree on Christmas Eve. I was hoping to be able to ride over to see Skylar the day after Christ-

mas to give her present to her, but I was going to have to wait and see about that.

Chapter 7

On Christmas Eve everyone was in a festive mood. The women shooed us men out of the house while they cooked and baked all day. When we were finally allowed back in to eat a quick, delicious dinner and get dressed to go to church, I couldn't help but enjoy how wonderful the house smelled.

Even though we dressed in our nice Sunday clothes, it really wouldn't have made any difference. No one would be able to see them beneath the heavy coats, hats, gloves, and even the blankets Mom had us wrapped in for the ride to and from church.

Calvin and I rode on the bench with Dad while everyone else cuddled up in the back of the wagon and we all sang Christmas carols in between sips of the hot coffee in our thermoses. Our church is only six miles from our house, so the trip took a little less than two hours, which seemed incredibly fast after traveling four or more hours everywhere we wanted to go.

We could see from a half mile away that there were indeed people at the church – it was all lit up with candles and we could see shadows of people walking and standing in front of the windows. We were excited to see friends again, some of which we hadn't seen since the Sunday before PF Day.

When we arrived, we were surrounded and greeted warmly, everybody acting especially nice to Robin as they expressed their sympathy at the loss of her father. Apparently, despite the distances between farms, the Jenkins's had spread the word and Robin was made into a bit of an unwilling VIP that night. Even with the food shortages, people had brought gifts of canned and baked goods for Robin and our family. We all felt immensely loved and cherished and full of the spirit of the season. It seemed even our circumstances couldn't stop Christmas.

After a beautiful service, during which the entire congregation had to cuddle together for warmth, my family and I climbed back into our wagon to make the journey home. We gave a ride to a couple, Johnny and Crystal Phillips, and their two young daughters, who live on the way to our house and had walked the mile and a half to the church. We sang Christmas carols again, with them joining in until we let the family off at their house. Mrs. Phillips invited us in to get warm by their fireplace and drink a cup of hot tea before we took off again. We were all quiet after that, and Calvin, Robin, and Granny even fell asleep before we got home.

We decided to wait until morning to open presents since we were all wasted from the long trek in the cold night air. We went to bed, but Alex snuck out of my room after a while to be with Robin. I had a little trouble sleeping after that until Alex came back a couple of hours later. I didn't ask what he had been up to; I was pretty sure I already knew

In the morning, we all gathered around the fireplace in the family room as usual, sipping coffee while Mom, Robin, and the grandmas made and baked homemade cinnamon rolls in the Dutch oven. The smell drove us crazy, and we almost burned our tongues devouring them as soon as they came out of the fire.

Mom told us kids to open our presents first, and we all had a good chuckle about the video games and movies she had bought us before PF Day. We were hopeful that we would be able to use them before too long. She, Robin, and the grandmas had also made each of us a dozen of our favorite type of cookie, although she said we were about out of flour and sugar now.

Alex gave Calvin and me some of his old belongings that we had wanted, like his Xbox 360 and video games. He said he wouldn't need them anymore, even when the power came back on, because he was getting too old for those kinds of things. He looked at Robin and put his arm around her shoulders when he said it. Even though we couldn't use the video games right then, the fact that he had given us something of his we had always wanted made it special.

Calvin gave me an elaborately drawn certificate worth two weeks of math homework, which Mom frowned at and then laughed at. I gave Calvin a cartoon drawing of us riding horses side by side. Dad gave each of us boys a hundred dollars and told us to save it for when we could go shopping again. Papa gave us each fifty dollars more and chuckled while saying, "Don't spend it all in one place, now."

Then, it was time for Calvin and me to give out our presents. We handed Granny and Gram and Papa a large wooden plaque, on which we had engraved "Home Sweet Home" to hang in their common room. They oohed and ahhed over it until we were a little embarrassed, although we were proud of ourselves at the same time.

We had made Alex and Robin a plaque that read "First Christmas Together," to which Robin started crying, a big smile on her face that was matched only by Alex's. For Dad, we all went out to the barn. Calvin and I had cleaned up the old steel buhr mill used to crack corn for chicken feed and attached it by a belt to an old bicycle whose tires were flat. We had made a stand for it to keep it stationery so that, when you rode the bike, it turned the crank on the mill, making grinding grain that much easier. It would come in handy in grinding wheat for flour or corn for cornmeal now that we were almost out. Dad was beaming with pride, but I don't know if it was pride in his new gadget or pride in his resourceful sons. I hoped it was both.

We saved Mom's gift for last. Everyone filed back into the kitchen, and Calvin and I dragged it – still covered in the blanket – out of the utility room. Mom uncovered it to find a homemade washing machine.

Laundry was such a chore for her; she had been leaning over the bathtub after pouring boiled water over the clothes, then rubbing each piece of clothing together until they came clean. She then had to rinse them several times with more boiled water. It took her nearly an entire day at least once a week, and at the end of the day her hands were red and cracked and sore.

Calvin and I had made a washing machine of sorts from a five gallon plastic bucket with holes in the bottom and a paddle fashioned out of an old oar stuck through a hole in the lid. This bucket was placed inside another five gallon bucket. We had found a big mop pail in the barn, the kind with the roller wringer on top, and we placed it and the buckets in a small, oval, metal tub that was once used for water for the goats. Mom still would have to boil the water for it, but she could now keep her hands out of the hot water for the most part. After agitating the clothes with the paddle, she had only to lift the first bucket out of the bottom one, allowing the water to drain out through the holes, empty the bottom bucket and refill with clean water, and place the top bucket back in to rinse the clothes. Then, she could remove the lid and paddle, dump the clean, but soaking wet, clothes into the mop bucket and feed each piece of clothing through the rollers to wring them out.

Mom was so happy that she began to cry. Robin went over and hugged her, saying, "You so deserve this."

Maybe it was the emotional moment that prompted him, but Alex then took Robin's hand and led her to the fireplace, where he asked for everyone's attention. "Robin and I have an announcement to make," he said.

Everyone held their breath; I think we all were expecting them to announce that Robin was pregnant or something, but instead, he said, "Last night, I asked Robin to marry me and she said yes." He tenderly gave her a kiss on the forehead.

After a long, stunned silence, Mom recovered enough to say, "That'll be great in a couple of years, but you're both only seventeen now."

"I'll be eighteen next month," Alex countered. "And Robin will be eighteen in March."

"Still, that's so young," Mom replied.

"Mom, we love each other and we want to be together. What difference does it make if it's in a month or a year?"

"So many things can change in a year," Mom argued. "When the power is back on and you both go back to school, you may feel different."

"We've been in love for over a year, Mom, and that was when we were at school and the power was on. That's not going to change."

Dad cleared his throat then and said, "I think this is happy news. I'll be proud to call you my daughter, Robin. Whether you get married now or later, we'll decide after Christmas. For now, I'm ready for the delicious meal you lovely ladies have prepared for us."

Everyone agreed wholeheartedly, so we all gathered around the dining room table downstairs to eat our feast of ham, homemade rolls, canned green beans and fried onions, and homemade apple pie. There weren't as many dishes as we usually had at the holidays but, for some reason, the dinner tasted better than any meal we'd ever had.

I can't remember a Christmas that was more special and happy before that one.

Chapter 8

In January, it got cold – bitterly cold. And it snowed – a lot. It seemed like we were having to pay Mother Nature back for the nice weather she had given us in November and December. Our deep freeze in the garage was starting to get low on meat, so my brothers, my Dad, Robin and I decided to go hunting. Paying heed to the Guardsmen who had visited the month before, we left our guns at home and hunted with bows instead.

We only had three bows, so we had to take turns. We figured that the hunting season laws would have been suspended because of the power failure and the number of starving people, but we weren't sure. At any rate, we doubted that any conservation agents were working at this time or that they had transportation to get around to everyone's farm to make sure they were obeying the law.

Dad said normally he would never break the law, but since martial law had been declared it had probably changed everything anyway. And he reminded us what the Guardsmen had said: desperate times call for desperate measures. We hadn't gotten desperate yet, but we could be only a blizzard away from desperation at any time, and it was always best to be prepared for the worst.

We stayed pretty warm and cozy in the house with the fireplace and the woodstove burning 24/7, but outdoor activity was kept at a minimum, except for the days we went hunting. That meant going to see Skylar was out of the question. Even if Mom had let me go (which she wouldn't have) I would have frozen to death by the time I reached town. Maybe I could have been caught in a snowstorm, too. Even I was not too keen on chancing that.

I hid Skylar's Christmas present in my room to save for when I could see her next. I hadn't seen her in several weeks and it was driving me crazy. Every time I saw Alex and Robin holding hands or hugging and kissing, I thought of Skylar. Every time Alex snuck out of my room in the middle of the night to be with Robin, I thought of Skylar. Every time I dreamed, I dreamed of Skylar, and even when I daydreamed, I daydreamed of Skylar. Sometimes I thought I had the image of Skylar burned into my retinas like an image left too long on a computer screen.

One day, when Calvin, Alex, Robin, and I were out hunting together – Dad had stayed home to fix some downed fence wire on the horse paddock – I twisted my ankle really bad. Calvin and I were by ourselves, trying to flush out rabbits in a big pile of brush by the creek, when a huge turkey jumped out at me from the undergrowth. It startled me and I fell back, slipping on a loose branch underfoot. Calvin burst out laughing, which probably scared away all the game for miles around, and I chuckled at my clumsiness, as well. That is, until I tried to stand up. The sudden pain in my ankle took my breath away and I fell back down on my butt, wincing. One look at my face told Calvin that I was in serious pain, so he laid down his bow and ran to my side.

Calvin tried to help me stand, but even leaning against him with my hurt ankle in the air was excruciating, and I couldn't stop the tears from forming in my eyes. I sat back down while Calvin began calling for Alex to help. Alex and Robin were quite a ways away, but they came crashing through the brush as fast as they could. Robin took off her long scarf and wrapped it tightly around my ankle. Alex and Calvin then picked me up, one on each side of me, with their arms linked under my butt and my knees. They carried me home that way, and it must have taken the better part of an hour to get back. Robin ran ahead to alert my parents, and the three of them met us as we were coming up the back pasture.

Dad took me from my brothers and carried me all the rest of the way to the house on his own. I had always known that Dad was strong, but I didn't realize he was that strong at the age of forty-three. He wasn't even breathing hard when he laid me on the sofa in the family room and pulled it closer to the fireplace.

Mom took over then, gently pulling off my hiking boots and socks while I bit my lip to keep from yelling, then giving the ankle a quick examination. She decided that I needed to take my jeans off, as well, and that hurt, too, even though she was very careful. I took off my coat, hat, and gloves, and Robin brought me a heavy quilt to curl up in.

Mom asked her to make me some hot tea and told her to use the dried willow bark in it. She also told her to steep some dried comfrey leaves in a bowl with a little bit of boiling water to make a poultice for my ankle. She put a pillow under my foot and made me lie there all day while she and Robin waited on me and doctored me. I know Mom was concerned about me, but it seemed like she was almost enjoying the chance to use her new knowledge about herbal medicines.

Everyone took turns sitting and talking with me for a while, and the rest of the day went by mercifully fast as a result. I slept on the couch that night and stayed there all the next day. Mom alternated the warm comfrey poultices with snow packed on my ankle every half hour.

The biggest problem I had while my ankle healed was getting to the bathroom. Someone had to help me get there for the first couple of days (not the most comfortable situation, I can tell you); after that, I could hop on one foot to get there.

Let me explain here how we had to handle the toilet situation after PF Day. We had to use a bucket of water poured in the stool to flush it. That meant a lot of going out to the hand pump to fill buckets of water in order to flush two toilets with nine people using them. We soon adopted the "if it's yellow, let it mellow" policy to save on water hauling.

Another problem that presented itself in

the bitterly cold month was the outdoor hand pump freezing up. Dad had to build a little house for it lined with leftover batt insulation from when we insulated our attic. Even then, there were mornings when he had to go out with a lit branch and unfreeze it with the fire. We started filling every bucket we had on the premises with water during the afternoon, which was the warmest part of the day, and keeping them in the family room all night so we'd have water to use that evening and the next morning.

Hauling water was a chore no one really liked to do, but everybody knew was important. It was usually up to us boys to fill all the buckets every afternoon, and with all three of us doing it, we usually got it done pretty quickly, but boy, was it cold!

I felt really bad for the three weeks or so that it took my ankle to heal enough to walk on. It was another couple of weeks before I could carry the heavy buckets of water without hurting my ankle under the pressure. But Robin, sweet Robin, willingly took my place at the pump for all those weeks.

It hadn't taken long for all of us to see why Alex loved her. She was so sweet and caring and you could tell she wasn't just doing it for "brownie points". I didn't know how everything was going to work out after the power was turned back on, but for the time being, we were all glad to have Robin. She was getting especially close to Mom – she was the daughter Mom had never had, and Mom was the mother Robin couldn't remember.

Mom and Robin also shared an interest in herbalism and studied the books Mom had gotten daily. They tended their herbs and talked about them all day. They were constantly on the lookout for aches, pains, sniffles, and coughs that they could doctor. The funny thing was, though, besides my sprained ankle, no one in our house got sick or hurt that winter. We had always had a bout of the flu and several rounds of colds during the winter months, but that year, not a sniffle. Mom said it was probably due to the fact that we were not exposed to any viruses since we had seen no one outside our family since Christmas Eve. It seemed strange, but it was nice to wake up feeling strong and healthy every day.

I caught up on a lot of schoolwork while I was off my feet. It's not that I really wanted to do it, but I can tell you, it gets pretty boring without TV or video games when everyone is off doing something else. I couldn't even listen to music. Sometimes I would hobble downstairs to visit my grandparents, but I mostly kept to the couch or my bed and read or did schoolwork.

Whenever I had trouble with a geometry assignment, Calvin would help me out. I think he might be a teacher when he grows up, because he always had a way of explaining things that made them unbelievably easy to understand. It also helped that I could go at my own pace and spend more time on things I didn't quite get. I wasn't under the pressure of school. At home, I found myself truly learning.

Mom helped me with history by sitting and talking with me about a particular period I was studying. Sometimes Alex and Robin would join us, and we would have lively discussions about the Hundred Years War or the French Revolution and we would repeat, "Let them eat cake!" and other famous sayings any time a chance presented itself. It was fun learning history that way, even more so because we could now really understand the hardships of living during that time period.

For science, Dad read up on some cool experiments that he, Alex, Calvin, and I would try to recreate at our kitchen table.

Some worked great while others kind of flopped, but I think I learned more from those experiments than I had in any science class. It was a hell of a lot more fun anyway.

English had always been a piece of cake for me. Mom had me writing stories and poems and, of course, reading, reading, reading. By the time the power came back on, I was sure I would be the best-read kid at school. Mom had checked out dozens of classics and some more modern books from the school library. I liked to read. It was a way to escape my boredom and the throbbing in my ankle for those first couple of weeks. After that, I was so addicted to it, I couldn't stop reading except to do my chores and other schoolwork. It also helped keep my mind off Skylar.

I hadn't seen her for almost two months and it was horrible. I wondered if she was thinking of me, or if she had decided I lived too far away to mess with. It was the worst feeling, being left to wonder if she was making out with some guy in town. I also worried about her getting enough water and food and staying warm enough without burning down her house.

Alex and Robin's happiness together didn't help the situation, and although I was glad for them, I had to look away when they got all lovey-dovey. I was so looking forward to spring, when we could take the wagon to town and I could see Skylar and get all my questions answered. There was her Christmas present, too, although I was thinking I should be calling it a Valentine's Day present instead.

I tried hinting to Dad about wanting to go to town as soon as we could "to get supplies" and he said we would when the weather lets up a bit. He said it with a twinkle in his eye that made me think he was on to me wanting to see Skylar. Dad was quiet but he didn't miss much that went on around him. He was a pretty cool dad. As long as you acted like a gentleman and did your part around the house and farm, he'd help you out whenever he could. After Robin lost her dad, I was more and more thankful that I still had mine.

Chapter 9

By March, spring had still not arrived, but the worst of winter seemed to be over. February had been as brutal as January, so we only got the wagon out once that month, and that was to go check on Mr. and Mrs. Caruthers. Aside from Mrs. Caruthers being all bent up with pain from her arthritis, they were faring pretty well. Mom had made up some tea of dried alfalfa and celery seeds with instructions for Mrs. Caruthers to treat her arthritis. We then chopped more wood for them and checked on their livestock.

Mrs. Caruthers gave us jars of gooseberries, stewed tomatoes, and applesauce that she had canned in the fall. "Gotta make sure you get enough vitamin C," she said. "Wouldn't want to get scurvy now, honey."

Speaking of honey, she gave us three big jars of honey from her nephew who raises bees in the next county over. We had run out of sugar shortly after Christmas, so that honey tasted amazing. Besides making sure Mr. and Mrs. Caruthers were all right, the honey made the freezing cold trip worth it.

Not much else happened until the middle

of April, when spring finally began getting the upper hand in the wrestling match with winter. One chilly but sunny day, Dad decided we should all ride into town. You can bet we were more than excited. Even the grandparents wanted to go.

Dad loaded up the truck with buckets of grain and smoked venison, leaving just enough room for everybody to sit. Mom tucked us all in with blankets and thermoses of the last of our coffee, along with a picnic lunch of deer jerky, Mrs. Caruthers' applesauce, and a handful of honey cornmeal cakes that Mom had made. The trip there may have seemed excruciatingly long, but I think the horses were as excited as we were, clipping along at a good speed the entire way. We made it in three hours instead of the usual four.

The first thing we noticed as we approached the town was that the four huge windmills were turning, their immense, whale-fin blades lazily slicing through the air. They had been still the last few times we'd visited, and the sight gave us hope that power may be back on in the town. We noticed when we got into town, however, that there were no lights on and businesses were still closed. There was no one in the town square. It seemed there was no one in the rest of the town, but as we plodded around, we came upon a group of kids and asked them what was going on. I was disappointed to find that Skylar wasn't among the group.

They told us that the trading market that used to be held in the square had been moved to the school gym for the winter and that most of the townspeople were gathered there. When asked about the windmills, the kids enthusiastically explained that parts had been obtained, and that the electric company had just recently been able to test them.

With a renewed sense of excitement and hope, we rode to the school and joined what seemed like half the town in the gym. I hadn't seen that many people packed into the gym since we won our district basketball game last school year. The president of the Electric Co-op, Mr. Jenkins – Mom's boss – was trying hard to be heard above the din of excitement in the crowd.

Everyone was hopeful that they would have electricity soon, but Mr. Jenkins explained that it may be a gradual process and that the windmills would probably not be enough to run everything in the town. Priority would be given to getting water and heat on for those that were in greatest need.

Then, his team would work on getting at least a little power to everyone else. He warned us to unplug all appliances, including furnaces and air conditioners, and to make sure all light switches were off so that when the electricity came back on, the surge wouldn't blow anything out.

After Mr. Jenkins finished answering questions from the crowd, everyone came down out of the stands and started milling around. There was a lot of laughter and patting friends on the backs. I spotted Skylar's parents from across the gym and headed their way, hoping she would be with them.

Mrs. Tipton spotted me looking around and hollered, "Bracken, honey," – she always called me and almost every other customer "'honey" – "are you looking for Skylar?"

I was surprised that she knew what I was doing and a little worried that I was so transparent in my intentions, but when I nodded yes, she pointed over to the first row of the stands where Skylar was sitting rather forlornly, looking down at her hands in her lap, all by herself. I tried to saunter over there coolly, but I couldn't help myself and I ended up rushing over, probably looking like Leroy Jenkins of World of Warcraft fame charging into battle.

Skylar looked up at me before I got to her, and the smile that spread across her face was enough to light up the whole town. She jumped up and threw her arms around me, almost knocking me off my feet.

"Brack!" she exclaimed. "I've been so worried about you, all alone out there in the country!"

I wasn't sure if she was thinking that my parents hadn't returned, since they were away from home the last time she'd seen me, or if she meant my being alone without her. I started to say that I'd been worried about her, too, but she grabbed my hand and said, "Let's get outta here!"

We snuck out of the gym and found a spot on the south side of the building that was shielded from the north wind. Skylar immediately cuddled up to me and my fears of her finding someone else were instantly put to rest. With my arms around her waist, I could tell she was even thinner than she had been the last time I'd seen her, when I had ridden behind her on Jenny Garten's horse. It made me very concerned about her and I asked her how she'd been.

"The winter was awful," she replied sadly. "It was really hard getting food and water because of the snowstorms." Then with tears in her eyes, she added, "Lots of people died, Brack. It was so horrible. We couldn't even bury them until last month."

She recited a list of names of the people who had died, mostly elderly people who I didn't know well, but there was one that shocked me to the core: Irvine Smith.

She said he'd suffered so much since he couldn't get any of the drugs he was addicted to, and his health had just continued to fail. He didn't have a very good family and, at one point, they had even thrown him out of the house. He had stayed with various families in the town, but in January he was found outside, frozen to death after a snowstorm. No one was sure if he committed suicide or if it was an accident. Even though Irvine wasn't a close friend of mine, I was shaken by the sadness of the situation and the fact that he had been friendly to me the last time I'd seen him.

"Did you hear about Robin's dad?" I asked Skylar after I had regained my composure.

"Yeah, Mr. Jenkins told everyone not long after it happened. How's Robin doing now?"

"She's doing pretty well. She's been a

lot of help around our house." I paused and studied her face. "Did you hear that she and Alex are getting married?"

"You're kidding!" she exclaimed. "Are your parents letting them?"

"Well, they said it would be fine in another year or so," I answered. "Oh, by the way, I made you a Christmas present. I guess I can give it to you for an early birthday present, even though it's a month away." I reached in the pocket of my insulated coat and pulled out her gift, wrapped in paper on which I had drawn figures of horses. It looked kind of childish, but Skylar grabbed it out of my hand and squealed in delight.

"Merry Christmas, happy Valentine's Day, and happy early birthday, Sky," I said with a nervous laugh.

"Oh, it's so beautiful!" she gushed. "That's the prettiest wrapping paper I've ever seen! Did you draw this? It's so good!"

"Well, don't get too excited. I didn't have much to work with," I said, embarrassed, while she unwrapped the package, being careful not to rip the paper. As she held the object in her hand, she whispered, "Ohhh," and then was silent for a few moments as she looked at it.

I wasn't sure if she was disappointed or touched, but then she clasped it to her heart and looked at me with tears in her eyes. Then, she put her arms around me and held me tight, whispering in my ear, "It's the most beautiful thing I've ever seen. Thank you."

I had carved her a tiny galloping horse out of a piece of wood I'd found in the barn. The way two of its legs came together at the bottom formed a softly rounded heart in the open space under its belly. I had painted it with cherry stain to make it match the reddish brown of Jenny's horse and rubbed it all over with Tung oil so it was smooth and shiny. Then, I had fashioned a little wire loop that I screwed into its back and attached it to a delicate silver chain that Robin had given me when I told her what I was making. I thought it had turned out rather well, and I was pleased that Skylar seemed to love it.

I knew she loved it because of how she kissed me afterward. We made out for a long time, which was great, and then we just sat on the steps to the side door of the school and talked. Skylar told me more about how life had been in town during the winter. She said that a couple of guys in town, who were machinists by trade, had made dozens of homemade, wood-burning stoves out of old water heaters for the people who didn't have fireplaces in their houses.

Several farmers who lived on the out-skirts of town had loaded up 200-gallon truck tanks with water and brought them to town daily in wagons pulled by horses or mules. It got harder and harder to do in January and February because of the snow-storms and the sub-zero temperatures, so everyone had to melt snow for water in those few weeks.

Skylar said that everyone in the town was very kind and helpful toward one an-other. It didn't surprise me; our town had always been generous. She spoke of how everyone pitched in to try to keep the senior citizens warm and well fed, but they still weren't able to save many of them. Again, I was struck by how lucky I was to have all my family, including my grandparents, alive and well.

Skylar also said that last week, an army truck had arrived with the parts needed to replace some transformers and fix the windmills. The soldiers had told the towns-people that electricity was gradually being restored to most of the cities and even some of the smaller towns like ours. Unfortunately, though, they said it could take another couple of months before electricity could reach those of us living in the country.

That was all right, though. I was kind of getting used to life without power and even starting to like it. It was hard to imagine going back to the way things were before, going back to school and wasting our lives away playing video games and watching TV. I had a feeling that I wouldn't be so dependent on those kinds of entertainment even if I had them literally at my fingertips. I have to say, that was a good feeling.

According to the soldiers, the country, and probably the rest of the world, was in financial ruin because of the solar superstorm. I had never thought about it, but our nation had virtually stopped, in terms of manufacturing and business, for almost six months. World markets had collapsed and most countries would be bankrupt after this. The only good thing was that, since virtually every country was in the same boat, there could be a chance to wipe the slate clean, in a sense, and start rebuilding the treasuries.

That day was the first time I heard the name "PF Day." Skylar said that was what the soldiers had called the day of the solar superstorm – short for Power Failure Day. I didn't think it was a very clever term, but it is descriptive, at least. It's also easy to say, easy to remember, and easy to write. The name is growing on me.

Skylar took me to her house for a cold lunch of canned pork and beans. It was odd that Mr. and Mrs. Tipton hadn't been cooking anything since they closed the diner. Skylar explained that they hadn't had the heart to cook for just the three of them. They'd been living on the few cans of food they had left from the diner. That explained Skylar's weight loss. I hoped that the return of electricity would restore the Tiptons' enthusiasm for cooking, both for their sakes and for the sake of everybody who liked to eat at their diner, including me.

I had promised Mom and Dad that I would meet them back at the wagon by two o'clock so we could get home before dark. Skylar assured me that she and Jenny would ride the horses out to our house as soon as they could, and I said I'd try to borrow one of our own horses to come see her, too.

To my amazement, she said, "Bring Calvin, too. I think Jenny kind of likes him." Who would have thought that a sophomore in high school would like an eighth grader? I mean, it was only two years apart, and it's true that Calvin was smarter than most of the sophomores in our school, but still.

I didn't want to leave Skylar and she didn't want to let me go either, but after an intense make-out session in the shed behind her house, I left to join my family at the school. There were still many people trading food and supplies in the gym. Mom and Dad had been able to trade some of our stuff for some farm supplies, but there was very little to be had in the way of food or necessities like toilet paper.

In the end, Dad donated quite a bit of grain to people who were hungry. He said that he didn't want to haul it back home, but everyone knew he was just being generous. When I asked him about it later, he just smiled and said, "What goes around comes around."

I'd heard that phrase before, but it wasn't until just then that I figured out the true meaning of it. As I said before, my Dad is quite a guy.

Chapter 10

Things started happening kind of fast after our visit to town. First, we started seeing cars whiz by on the highway in front of our house again – one or two a day at first, and then gradually increasing to a dozen or more a day. A couple of people from town – friends of my Mom and Dad – came out to visit us in their cars and told us that some places in town had electricity again, including Riley's Gas Station. A gas tanker had even driven from Kansas City and filled the gas station's tanks so people could buy gas again. Even so, the price was higher than anything we'd ever seen before – $8 a gallon, over twice what it was before PF Day!

Other businesses were able to open back up in town, like the banks, so people could now get some of their money out, and the grocery store, although they still didn't have much to sell. The Electric Co-op was open, too, but Mom had decided not to go back to work and had given Mr. Jenkins her resignation when we were last in town. I was particularly excited to hear that Tipton's Diner had reopened and were serving a limited number of dishes while waiting for more supplies to arrive.

The phone company was open, but there were many repairs that needed to be done to get the phone lines back to working order. This was accomplished in a couple of weeks and I soon got the first phone call to the house in almost six months – it was from Skylar.

The week before my birthday, which is May 15th, I woke up before dawn one morning because of a strange glow beside me. It was my alarm clock, which I had forgotten to unplug.

The electricity was on!

I flipped the light switch to my room and then ran through the house, switching on lights and hollering to everybody that the electricity was back on. Everyone jumped out of bed, and the first thing Mom did was turn on the faucet, but Dad had to go out to the well and reset the pump. When the water was on and had run for several minutes to get the air and gunk out of the line, Mom plugged in the microwave and warmed up some water to make tea. We then all sat around, drinking our tea and wondering what would happen next.

Would we have to go back to school?

Would Granny and Gram and Papa move back to the assisted living apartments? Would all of our hard work fixing up the wood stove, the place for the horses, the cooking grate for the fireplace, the bicycle-powered mill, and the homemade washing machine be wasted? Would we keep the horses and the wagon? The sudden change was harder to get our heads around than PF Day had been.

After we drank our tea and ate some breakfast, Dad turned on the TV and, though it came on, there was no signal, only an annoying static sound. Alex turned on a radio instead and got a scratchy signal of a station playing some country song. We all gathered around it, amazed to hear music again. We listened for a while and then left it on while we went about our chores.

The return of electricity didn't make too much of a difference in our lives those first few days, except for the fact that we didn't have to pump water or pour water in the toilet to flush it. Mom benefited the most from having the power back, because now she could use the dishwasher, washing machine, stove, microwave, toaster, and the vacuum cleaner. If we'd had any coffee, she could have used the coffeepot, too, and just the idea that she could made her and Dad mighty thirsty for coffee.

The refrigerator would come in handy, too, with the coming warmer weather. I must say that having the furnace back on was kind of strange. We had gotten used to dressing warmly in the house and having the temperature at 60°, so it seemed awfully hot inside. We decided to turn off the furnace to save money and just burn our firewood until it was warm out.

We were lucky, I know; we had money in the bank and plenty of grain to sell when we got enough diesel fuel for the semi to haul it. We had proven to ourselves for the past six months that we could be totally self-sufficient without too much hardship. Lots of people weren't so lucky. Many businesses had gone bankrupt during the shutdown, and others had to spend so much money to re-open that they didn't have enough to pay their entire workforce, so there were hundreds and hundreds of layoffs.

I heard that the two machinists, who had kept so many people warm by making them wood-burning stoves, were laid off, but everyone in town was supporting them and their families. Many people lived from paycheck to paycheck and, without having a paycheck

111

for several months, they didn't have money to buy groceries or gas or to pay their bills.

A big question on everyone's minds was if they would have to repay the banks for the months they couldn't pay their mortgages. Our old farmhouse and the 840 acres it sits on had been in my Dad's family for years, so we didn't owe anything on it. Skylar said that her family was in fairly good shape, too, however, they had a mortgage on the house and their restaurant, so her parents were worried about having to pay the past-due mortgage amounts.

On my birthday, my 16th birthday, Gram and Granny made me a special, made-from-scratch chocolate cake and, boy, did it taste good. They had to use the whole-wheat flour that Dad ground on the bicycle-powered mill and honey from Mrs. Caruthers' son since there still wasn't much in the way of groceries to buy, but it tasted great anyway.

I didn't get a lot of presents, considering there weren't many stores open to buy gifts from, but Dad let me drive the car to town with some of the gasoline he had saved and we all ate lunch at Tipton's Diner. That was the best present I could have imagined. Skylar waited on us, and then her parents let her go with me to the school to get re-registered so I could start back the next week. It seemed weird being at school again, but I was happy and proud to be seen with Skylar hanging on my arm.

Alex, Robin, and Calvin had to re-register for school as well. Alex tried to convince Mom and Dad that he should just drop out of school and stay home to help Dad on the farm, but they wouldn't have it. Dad said Alex would need to get an Ag degree in college if he wanted to be a competitive farmer these days, and that meant staying in school. Mom said she'd hate to have one of her sons be a dropout. Finally, Robin talked him into going so she wouldn't have to be alone. Of course, she wouldn't really be alone – Calvin and I would be riding to school with her – but I'm sure she meant without Alex.

The school counselor explained that we might have to go to school through the summer unless Congress decided to make a special waiver for the number of days required for us to attend that particular school year. I sure didn't want to have to do that!

I mean, it would have been nice to see Skylar every day, but it would have been even nicer to see her anywhere other than school. We told the counselor that we had carried on with our schooling at home during the winter, and she was very pleased to hear that. She said that she wished every parent had had the foresight to do that; then we could just say we'd been homeschooled for six months, and all could go back to normal.

That got me thinking about being homeschooled. Now that Mom wasn't working, I wondered if she would consider it. I had really enjoyed it while we were at home that winter, and I was sure that Alex and Robin would jump at the chance; maybe even Calvin. The only problem was that Skylar would be at school all day, miles away from me.

After we registered, I walked Skylar back to the diner. Skylar needed to stop by her house on the way, and she came out holding a small box and an envelope. She handed them to me and said, "These are for you. Happy birthday, Brack."

I started to open the envelope first, but she stopped me and said, "Open that at home." Then, she put her hand on mine and added shyly, "When you're alone."

That really intrigued me and made me want to open it right then, but I promised her I'd wait. Instead, I opened the small box to find a religious token on a silver chain. I was kind of confused. I never knew Skylar and her family were Catholic; I didn't even think they were very religious at all.

I must have had a strange look on my face because she quickly explained, "It's St. Valentine, the patron saint of lovers."

I grabbed her and kissed her then and we made out for a while before she had to leave to get back to the diner.

That evening, we ate at Tipton's again – I said it was all I wanted for my birthday – and Dad let me drive home afterward. When we got home, Dad flipped on the TV as he had been doing every night to check for any programming, and we were excited to have a couple of channels from Kansas City come in. They were showing reruns until nine o'clock, when a special news broadcast came on. We all gathered around the TV in the family room to watch since we hadn't seen any news about anywhere other than our county for months.

The news was grim. On PF Day, several planes had crashed because of the onslaught of geomagnetic particles disrupting their in- struments and the control towers. There were also many train wrecks, especially in countries with high-speed trains. With the crashes, the fires, the cold, the lack of food and water, and the lack of medicine, millions of people worldwide had died on or in the months following PF Day.

According to the latest count in Kansas City, there were at least 15,600 people dead from the power failure. And that was just Kansas City. We could only imagine what the total was for the entire country — or the world. One thing that really struck us as tragic was that there had been no contact with the astronauts on the International Space Station, and no one knew for sure if they were alive or dead. I don't know why that seemed more tragic than all the other terrible things, but somehow, the thought of them abandoned out in space seemed especially disheartening.

There were so many unknowns, like how long would it take for everything to be back to normal? When was the manufacturing industry going to get back online? When were stores going to start having products again? When would they get satellites back in space again, so we could have cell phones and satellite TV? When would they begin to drill for oil again and to refine it into gasoline? Would the banks and the stock markets collapse? Would we be in a depression?

There were too many questions that couldn't be answered yet.

After soaking in the news, I went to my room and locked the door. I didn't want Alex to come in while I was reading the card from Skylar. I won't reveal everything it said, but the gist of it was that she loved me. She said that I had changed her life. Imagine that – at a time when PF Day changed the world, she believed I was the one who had changed hers.

Despite the bad news on the TV, it had been a wonderful birthday.

Chapter 11

The next week, we started back to school. The school district couldn't afford the fuel for the busses, so it was up to each family to get their kids to school. A lot of people couldn't afford the gas either, so some of the families who lived outside of town decided to homeschool. Others rode their horses in, but only the ones who lived close enough. The school had to set up a place to keep the horses while we were in school. Since Mom didn't work in town anymore, Alex drove us to school in Mom's car.

It was so weird, sitting there in class and listening to the teachers and trying to act like everything was normal. We all knew it wasn't. Even the teachers found it hard to stay on topic. The classes often ended up talking about PF Day, what had happened since, and what might happen in the future. Our normal subjects just seemed so irrelevant now, and we struggled through until the end of the school year.

Congress approved the waiver that the counselor had talked about, so none of us had to attend summer school. The decision was more about the financial burden of keeping the schools open rather than any concern for us students, but who cared? We were off for the months of July and August. The school board also allowed most of the senior class to graduate since they had already completed all of their required courses, and that included Alex and Robin.

The only thing good about school, as I mentioned before, was seeing Skylar every day. For the first time in my life, I had a girlfriend. I was part of a couple. School made it a lot easier to see Skylar, but the summer break gave us even more freedom to really be together. Skylar and I both got our driver's licenses, and we still had access to horses when we couldn't borrow our parents' cars. It was fun to each ride our horses and meet halfway.

As for Jenny and Calvin, they didn't end up dating, but they were still friends and always came with us when we met by horse.

One new development that made me very happy was that my parents decided to let me start dating, and I mean going out on a date, as in taking the car and picking up Skylar to go out. Of course there wasn't really any place to go except Tipton's Diner and a pizza joint called The Dog House in another town a few miles away. We usually went there to eat and then drove down to the river and hung out with a few other couples. Skylar and I couldn't believe that her parents were letting her date, but she said they liked me and thought I was a nice kid. I guess they knew I'd keep her safe.

Dad was able to get a crop in the last two weeks of May. He was only able to get enough fuel to plant half of our acres. Alex and I helped him every day after school and on the weekends. He was also able to sell most of the grain he had stored from the last harvest and got a very high price for it. Unlike most Americans, we were doing okay money-wise, but the high cost of diesel and the fact that Dad could only plant half his usual acreage meant much lower profits for the year. We knew the harvest would be late this year, since we had planted a month late, and if the weather was bad in November and December it would make matters worse.

Mom decided that she wanted to build a greenhouse so she could start a home-based business growing and selling herbs and herbal remedies. Robin was very enthusiastic about it, too, and Mom said they could go into business together. It got Robin to thinking about studying herbalism in college. Dad and Alex helped them design and build a big greenhouse and a cold frame for them in an open field on the south side of the barn. It was really nice when it was done, and Mom and Robin got right to work planting herbs and making places to hang the harvested herbs for drying and work tables for preparing the herbal remedies.

Mom had traded some grain for a whole box of past issues of *Mother Earth News* at one of the trading markets in town and she and Robin had been reading them from cover to cover, finding all sorts of great information for living "off the grid" and being self-sufficient. Even though scientists didn't think we'd get another solar superstorm for a hundred years or so, Mom said that being informed never hurt anybody and there were a lot of other disasters that could deprive us of electricity.

Dad agreed with her about that and said, even if we still had electricity, to think about the money we could save by using the free energy from the sun. He found articles in the *Mother Earth News* magazines about building a solar water heater, a solar collector, and a solar bottle light bulb. When he was done with the greenhouse, he set to work on making them for our house, barn, and tool shed. He had us boys help him so we would learn how to do it. Calvin was especially intrigued and made some really cool design modifications to the plans that made them fit our situation better. He decided that would be a great science fair or 4H project for next year when he would be a freshman.

Our barn has a long side facing south with no doors or windows. We built two large solar collectors and attached them to that side of the barn. We built two smaller ones and attached them to the side of the house, one for heating the kitchen and the other for the living room. Basically, this heater is a flat, rectangular box, framed by 2x6s and attached to the south side of the building with a black wire mesh screen, or black piece of metal, on the back and a clear glass panel on the front. You then put a slot in the building both at the bottom and the top of the rectangle for the air to circulate over the heated surface and bring that heat into the building. If you've done it right, the sun is too high in the sky to strike the solar collector in warmer weather, but in winter, when the sun is low in the sky, the angle is perfect to warm it up. We weren't able to test them out since it was summer, but the chance would come soon enough.

Next, we built a solar water heater. It

was a trapezoidal shaped box lined with foam insulation, which has a reflective surface (Dad had to get this from a neighbor who had built a new house last year and had spare pieces left over). We got an old water heater tank out of our trash ditch and laid it on its side in the bottom of the box, then attached pipes to bring the water to and from it, and enclosed the top of the box with a double-paned glass from a sliding glass door (also salvaged from a neighbor). Calvin made the suggestion to add a connection for the cold-water intake to the outside pump so we could pump water to it without electricity. Like I said, Calvin was really into these projects.

Last, we added a quick and easy solar bottle light to the tool shed to light it without electricity. This was one cool and easy project. You take an empty, clear, two-liter soda bottle and fill it with distilled water and a little bleach to kill bacteria, and then fit it into a hole in the roof of the shed. There's a little more to it than that, but that's the basic idea. You would not believe the amount of light it brings into the shed. It glows just like a light bulb during the day and, except for the price of the caulk to seal it in the roof, it's free energy.

We were all really proud of our projects and it got us thinking about other ways to save money and improve things around the farm. Dad thought we should try to figure out a better way to pump water without electricity so we wouldn't have to go outside to do it. By the time we had started back to school right after Labor Day, the Internet was back up somewhat, although only some of the sites were available, and Dad was able to find plans for a hydraulic ram pump that uses only gravity and water to pump. He worked on that on his own, but we helped him connect it to the outside hand pump and run the pipe underground, in through the basement and up to the kitchen sink and to the solar water heater, as well. Dad also built a better shed for the whole works with it's own solar collector to keep it unfrozen in the winter.

Dad was spending every evening on the computer in his and Mom's bedroom searching the web. Calvin wondered if he was watching porn or something, but that wasn't in Dad's nature. You never know, though, so one day I got up the nerve to ask him what he was doing. He answered that he'd been bitten by the survival bug, whatever that meant, and he showed me some of the sites he was visiting and some of the plans he had downloaded. They were all ways to live "off the grid," that is, without electricity, and there were pages and pages of some *really* cool things – things I'd never even thought about.

Dad had printed off hundreds of sheets of plans, ideas, and information, hole-punched them, and put them into binders, all indexed and sorted. He had also gone through the *Mother Earth News* issues and torn out the pages that pertained to living without modern power and had included them in the binders, as well. He had one binder for building improvements, another for farming without petroleum products. In another binder, he had medical information, from first aid to medicine alternatives to emergency surgery techniques. In the fourth binder he had alternatives to food, cooking products, and cleaning supplies, like using roasted barley instead of coffee and how to make vegetable oil, candles, and soap. Lastly, he had a binder on animal husbandry – how to raise animals and use their prod-ucts. One thing he was especially interested in was how to raise bees for their honey. "I don't want to be without something sweet to eat," he told me with a grin. But then he went on to explain that honey is a powerful product for medicinal purposes, too. Its antimicrobial properties are great for treating coughs and sore throats, as well as an antiseptic for wounds.

We were pretty well set up for any event that we would lose electricity, like a storm, power plant failure, or even an act of terrorism. I had learned from one of my teachers that terrorists could, in theory, detonate a bomb above the U.S. and cause pretty much the same thing that the solar superstorm had. That was a scary thought.

Anyway, by the end of the summer break, Alex and Robin had registered for college and Calvin and I had to go back to school. Mom let Alex and Robin take her car to the university, which was 35 miles away, and I drove Calvin and me to school in Alex's car. Again, I found it hard to concentrate on my classes and this time it didn't have anything to do with Silky Henderson. After all, I was in a serious relationship and Skylar was all I could think about. I struggled to keep up my grades, but then so did everyone else. The teachers understood the problem and explained to us that we all had been through a very traumatic time, kind of like being in a war. They said it would take some time to get over it and they were pretty lenient that first month of school.

Chapter 12

On October 12 of that year, almost a year after PF Day, the unthinkable, the thing that scientists called a million to one chance, happened. It was on a weekend this time, so we were all at home. Dad and Alex were out in the field checking the corn that they hoped would be ready to harvest the next month, and Mom and Robin were in the greenhouse working with their herbs. The grandmas were tending the flowerbeds and Papa was lounging on the porch swing, joking with the ladies and giving them a hard time.

It was late afternoon and I was taking a shower, getting ready to go out with Skylar that night. Calvin had just come in and flipped on the TV to watch *Jeopardy*, which he was really good at. At some point, he started hollering something, but I couldn't quite make out what he was saying until I turned off the water. I'll never forget what he said or the sound of fear in his voice as he shouted it on his way outside to tell everyone else.

"Another one's coming! Another one's coming!"

I wasn't sure what the words meant exactly, but the sound of his voice told me enough. I ran to the TV and stood there, dripping wet and with nothing but a towel on, trying to absorb the news. Then suddenly, the TV popped and fizzled and the screen went blank.

Like the last time, I noticed right away the absence of the hum of electricity flowing through our lives. The silence was profound and I was scared. The last time this happened, we had had every reason to believe that electricity would be restored quickly. This time, I knew what was in store for us.

A crackle and loud pop brought me back to my senses, and I ran to my room to pull on some clothes. Then I ran downstairs, skipping three steps at a time, and out the back door.

The dogs were barking frantically down by the side of the barn. Mom and my grandparents were hurrying toward the barn, dragging the garden hose with them, while Robin was frantically pumping the hand pump to start the hydraulic ram pump. Once it had enough water pressure to start pumping on its own, Robin and I ran to the barn where Mom was spraying water at the small, drum-shaped transformer attached to a power pole, which was on fire near the corner of the barn.

A strange blue ripple of flame traveled down the power line toward our house as we all held our breath. Luckily, it went out before it got there. After the fire was out, we all stood around and hugged each other, with disbelief and worry reflected in each other's eyes.

Calvin had grabbed one of the horses in the paddock and had galloped toward the cornfield to find Dad and Alex. In a few minutes, Calvin rode up on the horse while Dad and Alex drove up behind them on the four-wheeler. They all had the same anxious look in their eyes. Even the horse was spooked, and he ran over to worriedly nuzzle his buddy when Dad put him back in the paddock.

All of us then went back into the house, where Dad turned on the battery-powered emergency radio to see if there were any stations still coming in. As he turned the dial up and down the face of the radio, it became obvious that the radio waves were disrupted, as well, as there was nothing but static.

The most important thing on my mind was Skylar. I ran to try the phone but, of course, it was dead, too. I stammered out some lame excuse to my family, "I – I mean we – need to go to town."

Again, Dad came through for me. "Yeah, we probably should go and see what we can find out."

Mom just shook her head. "I can't believe this is happening again. What are we going to do?"

Gram put her arms around Mom and said, "We did fine before and we'll do fine again, honey."

Mom cheered up a little then and we all got ready to go to town. We had to take both cars to fit us all in. We hated to waste the gas, but no one wanted to be left behind.

Everyone in town was in the same state of disbelief as we were. Some of the women were sobbing as we gathered once again in the town square. Skylar's mom was one of them. When I found Skylar, she was shaken but not crying. The thing she was most worried about was her parents' emotions.

"I don't know if they can take another one of these," she told me quietly. "They were so depressed before. The diner is their life, you know."

Robin was standing near us and overheard what Skylar had said. "With some help they could still run their diner," she offered. "I'm sure they had diners before electricity."

This cheered Skylar up immensely, and she hugged Robin. I also promised Skylar that our family would come help her family with the diner.

No one could understand why we had not been given more warning of the coming geomagnetic storm this time. Mr. Andresen and our other science teacher, Mr. Johnson, thought that maybe the space telescopes were not running at full capacity yet, or perhaps predicting such events relied on satellites, all of which were disabled by the last storm. In any case, we Midwesterners were not notified until minutes before it hit.

Skylar told me she had tried to call to warn us, but it must have been after I had gotten into the shower and right before Calvin had come in. It wouldn't have helped much anyway, but at least we could have tried saving the TV by turning it off. Now, it was probably fried.

The Aurora Borealis was in the northern sky again as the sun set, and the lights seemed even brighter than last year. The glow was so bright you could read by it, although it was like reading by flickering candlelight. They were also more red than blue-green this year.

On PF Day and for several days after, the lights had danced eerily in the night sky on every clear night, but had faded after a few days until they had been barely visible. I didn't see the beauty in them this time, only the omen of tragedy they foretold. Mr. Johnson wondered if they were brighter because the atmosphere had been compromised, a thought that was even more frightening.

I was reluctant to leave Skylar in town with her grieving parents, but she insisted she had to stay and take care of them. I promised I'd be back the next day, and every day thereafter, to help them prepare their house and the diner for the worst-case scenario – the electricity off for good. It seemed likely that things would be even worse, since there hadn't been enough time to manufacture goods such as transformers, and the strategic oil reserves used by the government to keep some semblance of order were almost used up.

Skylar and I held each other for a long time, right there in the square in front of our parents and everyone else, before I had to leave. She couldn't hold back the tears by the time I pulled away, and my own eyes were stinging.

Dad was worried about the harvest first and foremost. He had planted about 320 acres in corn, soybeans, and wheat. On another 30 acres, he'd grown a mixture of grasses, like timothy, brome, and rye, with some clover and alfalfa mixed in, for hay to feed our horses and to sell. He had also been experimenting with planting other grains and, on another 30 acres of tillable land, had planted oats and barley. He had been hoping to get enough fuel for the harvest before November, but hadn't been able to get more than enough to harvest a third to half of the crop. He knew now that getting any more was out of the question and he had to figure out how to harvest without fuel.

The next day, Dad took his farm pickup, to the Caruthers' house and brought us boys with him. I had wanted to go into town to help Skylar's family first thing in the morning, but Dad insisted that he needed my help first.

Mr. and Mrs. Caruthers were not nearly as upset by the absence of power as the rest of us were. Mr. Caruthers said that he'd always felt that life was better in the old days when people didn't rely on electricity. I guess that's why he collected what others thought of as junk, stuff that would be needed now to live a decent life. Dad was able to trade grain and the promise of physical labor for a horse-drawn reaper and a steam-powered thresher.

Mr. Caruthers asked Dad if he would be interested in taking over the rest of their livestock except for a couple of horses to pull their own wagon. They had a dozen horses, two mules, a couple of male donkeys, and two milk cows. Mr. Caruthers said it was just getting too hard for him to care for them, and he knew we would take good care of them. Dad agreed and said we would be back in a couple of weeks to get them. We would have to build more fences and stalls in the barn to keep all those animals.

After we had loaded the reaper into the bed of the pickup and the thresher onto the small flatbed trailer we'd brought along, we drove back to our house and unloaded them. Dad said that Calvin and I could go to town for the rest of the day to help Skylar's family, but we'd have to stay home and help build the fences for the next several days. I loaded up the trunk of Alex's car with firewood, some tools, and an axe, and we left without even eating lunch, instead taking a couple of sandwiches with us.

Skylar's house had one of those wood

stoves fashioned out of an old water heater that the machinists had made winter before. Her family had a few logs left over, but not nearly enough for the cold days ahead, so I gave them what I'd brought and promised to bring them more. Getting wood was not as easy for the townspeople as it was for us.

Calvin and I built the Tipton's a wood-pile that Dad would be proud of. Then, we went inside and fashioned them a flat metal surface and affixed it to the top of the wood stove to use as a cooking surface. I talked to Mr. Tipton about their food options and found that they were pretty low. I told him that I would try to keep them stocked in grain and hunted game this winter, but warned that he should probably think about another source, as well. He assured me that, though he hadn't hunted since he was a teenager because he was always too busy at the diner, some neighbors had offered to share game with them as much as possible in return for the Tipton's cooking it for them.

We discussed options for reopening the diner using non-electrical improvements, and Mr. Tipton started getting excited. He hollered for his wife to come in and listen while I told them about how we could add solar lighting to their dark kitchen and convert their big gas stove into a wood-burning one. It was so great to see the light come back into their dull, lifeless eyes, and I promised to come back with plans as soon as I could.

I got a little alone time with Skylar while Calvin continued talking to her parents about what they would need to do to reopen the diner. She was so happy that I had given her parents hope that she kept kissing me and hugging me tight. I told her she didn't owe me anything, but trust me, I enjoyed the enthusiasm.

We made out in her bedroom for over half an hour – I still can't believe her parents left us alone in there that long – before Calvin and I had to leave. I hated to have to tell her that it would be a few days until I could return, but she suggested coming to my farm to help us with the fence in exchange for more firewood. That seemed like the most awesome idea I'd ever heard, and it made me actually look forward to working on that fence the next day.

Chapter 13

For the next couple of weeks our lives were busy with preparing our place for the new livestock, getting the Caruthers' place ready for winter, and then bringing the animals home. Thanks to good weather, Dad and Alex were able to get almost half of the crop in with the combine by the end of November and began to use the horse-drawn reaper after that. By Christmas, they had finished the harvest, which was a massive relief. We would be okay for at least another year.

Skylar had been able to drive her parents' car to our place a couple of times in that first week, and then she and Jenny came on Jenny's horses at least twice a week afterward. The weather was beautiful – crisply cool but warm enough to be comfortable. When I got some free time, I rode one of our new horses, a black gelding that I particularly liked, in to town to see Skylar and work on the diner. Calvin usually tagged along, too, and we were able to install three solar tube lights in the diner's kitchen so that, at least in the daytime, they would have enough light to cook by. Mr. Tipton had already converted the gas stove to burn wood, saying he didn't even care if the change ruined it. Everyone was pretty sure that the power would be off for a long time; we had to begin adapting to life without it.

A week before Christmas, a couple of soldiers stopped by our house with one of those radiation detecting things – a Geiger counter, I think they called it – and walked around, testing the amount of radiation in the air around our farm. The thing kept clicking everywhere they went, and they said that the last solar superstorm had left behind more radiation in the atmosphere because the first one had blown away part of our magnetosphere, leaving us more exposed to radiation from the sun.

They told us that the worst exposure had been in the first couple of days, but even now it was best to stay inside, particularly in the basement, as much as possible. They also said to eat lots of foods that are high in antioxidants, like tomatoes, peppers, and broccoli. Mom smiled at that, turned to us boys, and said, "I told you that eating your vegetables would pay off sometime."

Before the soldiers left, they warned us again about marauders. The situation had gotten so bad in some places that gangs of starving people, mostly young men, were roving the countryside on foot and horseback, taking whatever they could get. In some instances, they had even killed to get what they wanted. They were also known to rape women and burn down houses just out of sheer spite and lawlessness.

That news shocked us, and Dad decided after the soldiers left that we needed to consider fortifying our home and protecting our resources, including our animals and the grain in our silos. That's the one thing about surviving that Dad hadn't downloaded any information on – defending ourselves against attack – and he said we would all need to brainstorm ways to keep away unwanted visitors.

Our closest neighbors were a middle-aged couple named Rick and Carla Thomas, who lived about two miles up the highway. They ran cattle on their acreage; not a huge herd, but about 40 head of cows and a bull. Dad figured that they might need some help in protecting their herd, and he and Alex rode to their house to talk about the idea of working together to protect our mutual interests.

That got Robin thinking about her Dad's herd of cattle, which she had given to the

Jenkins's to look after following the death of her father. At that time, she had wanted nothing to do with the animal that had killed her father, but now she started thinking about how having some of those cows would prove to be very useful. She decided that she and Alex would visit the Jenkins's and ask for a few head of cattle back.

On Christmas Eve, Mom sent me into town with the wagon to invite The Tipton's to spend Christmas with us. They were very touched by the offer, but explained that dozens of townspeople were counting on them to provide Christmas dinner, now that the diner was set up to run without electricity. Skylar begged her parents to let her go without them and they finally said she could, noting that it wouldn't be much of a Christmas for her if she had to spend the day waiting on customers at the diner.

It was arranged that she would stay two nights at our house so we wouldn't have to travel on Christmas. I assured them that she could sleep in Robin's room and she would be safe from any conceivable danger. Mrs. Tipton put her hand on my cheek and said, "We know. We trust you, dear." I blushed at her implication and had to turn away.

Skylar and I made it home before dark

and spent a long time together in the barn while putting away the wagon, brushing down the horses, and just talking. We knew we'd be hitching the horses back up to go to the candlelight service at church in a couple of hours, so we left them in their stalls. Our three dogs sat at Skylar's feet, gazing at her with the same adoration that I did, as she petted each in turn. Skylar had never had a dog, even though she adored them, so she gave each of mine tons of attention when she could. Even though we loved our dogs, they were farm dogs, outdoor dogs. They only got petted when we were outside and not busy, so the extra attention Skylar was giving them almost made them wiggle with excitement. She kind of had that effect on me, too.

We finally went in the house and had a nice dinner with my family, and then we all went to the candlelight service. I had such a strong feeling of déjà vu except that Skylar was holding my hand beside me in the pew.

Christmas day was wonderful, of course. It wasn't quite as special as that first Christmas without electricity, but it had its own special charm: the presence of Skylar.

The next day, I reluctantly drove her home in the wagon.

Oh, I almost forgot: the present Mom and Dad gave Alex and Robin was that they could get married on New Year's Eve, if they still wanted to. And of course they did still want to – more than ever! Alex asked me to be his best man and Robin asked Skylar to be her maid of honor. We had less than one week to get a wedding put together, but Mom already had a jump on it. She had been asking Robin all sorts of discreet questions about what kind of wedding she would like in the future, and she had secretly modified her own wedding dress to fit Robin's preferred style.

On New Year's Eve, Reverend Campbell came over to our house and married Alex and Robin in our family room. Only our family, Skylar, and the Reverend were there. I have to say, even though I've never cared for weddings and things like that, it was a really cool ceremony. I guess it's because Robin and Alex really loved each other and deserved to be together. I also benefited in two great ways: Skylar got to spend a couple of days at our house, and I got my room to myself again.

If it were Robin, or Skylar, or even Mom writing this, they'd probably go into great detail about the wedding, the flowers, the colors, what was said, how everyone reacted, etc., but honestly, I don't remember that much about the details.

I just remember that Robin looked beautiful in her long, white dress and her hair reminded me of a shiny new penny peeking out from under the veil in soft waves around her face. I remember that Alex was wearing a dark-colored suit and that he looked at Robin with such awe and devotion, it almost made me want to get married. Most of all, I remember Skylar, my beautiful, amazing Skylar, standing next to Robin, her honey-colored hair just brushing the shoulders of a satiny copper long dress just a couple of shades darker than Robin's hair, with a silver sash tied in a bow around her waist and another smaller version, in her hair.

She looked just like the most beautiful, wondrous present anyone could ever be given. As I stared at her, wishing I could tear open her wrapping – I know, not a very nice thought during such a solemn ceremony, but I couldn't keep my mind from wandering – she turned and smiled at me in a way that told me maybe her mind was already way ahead of mine on that train of thought. After that, I have no other clear memory of the ceremony, as I'm sure you can understand.

After Alex and Robin were married, we ate a big dinner of ham from a friend of Dad's who raises hogs, vegetables grown in Mom and Robin's garden, lots of homemade bread, rolls, and even a gooseberry pie, thanks to Mrs. Caruthers' jars of gooseberries.

We were all stuffed, but then Mom brought out a big box, which Skylar had brought with her when I picked her up. She had refused to tell me what was in it, saying it was a wedding gift from her family. Mom opened the box and lifted out a two-tiered white wedding cake with icing flowers all over it. We all oohed and ahhed over it then and again when we tasted it. Skylar told us that her mother had bargained with a few neighbors to collect enough sugar to make a real cake – I mean the sort of cake that we had taken for granted before PF Day.

Mom even brought out some Amaretto that she had stored somewhere in a cabinet and let all of us, even Calvin, have a little bit to ring in the New Year. That little bit was plenty for me. I've never really seen the point in drinking like a lot of the other kids in my school did. I mean, I don't really like the taste of alcohol and I've always been pretty happy with my life, so I don't feel like I need to drink to escape or to change who I am or even to prove myself. The guys I usually hung out with at school (before PF Day, of course) felt the same way, but we were more or less considered geeks and nerds for not going to any of the drinking parties.

Strangely, I didn't really miss my friends from school. That part of my life now seemed like ancient history, like I can just barely remember what we talked about or what we did back then. When I thought about friends on that special New Year's Eve, while we sang Auld Lang Syne and the part about old acquaintances and all, I realized that all the friends I would ever need were in the same room, all together: Mom, Dad, my grandparents, my brothers, Robin, and especially Skylar.

I also realized that PF Day and PF2 Day, as it came to be called, even with all the inconveniences and tragedies, had changed my life in ways I could never have imagined before, ways that made my family and me closer and more truly alive. I know that this probably sounds weird and maybe a little selfish, given all the misery other people had to endure, but that's what it did for our family, and, for the first time since PF Day, I was grateful for the loss of power.

Chapter 14

The second power failure seemed to be seen as more of a challenge to be won than the first time – when despair was the pervading emotion – to the people of our county. Although news had been trickling in from outside the United States that people were still suffering greatly, especially in the big cities, in Holt County there seemed to be a different spirit: "This is our lot, so let's make the best of it."

People really came together and started helping each other to carve a new life out of our circumstances, each person contributing resources, knowledge, skill, or just plain muscle to the good of the whole. Dad's knowledge of "off the grid" living techniques was an unbelievable resource for everyone, and made the transition to living without electricity much smoother and less painful. Through barter and trade – and a lot of charity of spirit, as Mom called it – everyone was taken care of and set up for surviving the winter.

The elderly, like my grandparents, also had a wealth of experience from their memories of life on the farm before electricity became so pervasive in our lives. Granny remembered helping her own Grandma make soap from ashes and hog fat. Papa knew how to butcher chickens. We had always had chickens, but they were more for egg laying and pets than for meat. Mom had always given all but one rooster away every spring when a new batch was born so she wouldn't have to butcher them. She said that chicken was just too cheap to buy in the store to go through the trouble and anguish of butchering her pets herself. But now, it was a necessity.

She felt the same way about her pet goats. She raised her goats for their milk and for the fun of seeing the rambunctious little babies born each spring. Like the roosters, Mom had always sold all but the one billy goat. Now, however, she knew she might have to have them slaughtered for their meat next fall.

Both of my grandmas knew how to milk a cow and remembered their grandmothers making butter from the fresh milk. Dad made a makeshift butter churn out of a five gallon bucket and another oar – much like the washing machine I had made Mom last year – and it wasn't long before we had mastered the use of it and began enjoying butter again. We had the goat milk and the cow milk and all the great things you can make from them, like cheese, yogurt, and butter, all of which Dad had downloaded instructions on how to make.

Dad traded grain for a hog right before Christmas and had us boys help him butcher it, while Papa instructed us from the memories of his childhood. It wasn't too different from butchering a deer, something my brothers and I had been doing since we were each ten or eleven years old, except that a hog is much bigger and heavier than a deer. Papa had to tell us how to cut it up into the various cuts of meat – the hams, chops, ribs, loins, bacon, etc. – and what to do with the leftover parts, all of which were useful for something.

The hooves and bones were kept for making gelatin, the fat for lard, the stomach and intestines for sausage casings. Even the brains were saved to be used in tanning the skin for making leather. Mom boiled the head, lungs, and other innards to make a rich broth, which she then canned and stored in the garage. Then, she rendered the fat – that is, boiled it until it became liquefied – to make lard for cooking and making soap. Later, Dad boiled the hooves and bones for several days until he had a pot of gelatin to be used for glue. We converted our tool shed into a smokehouse and smoked a huge amount of the meat to keep it from spoiling when the weather warmed up.

People in town started to specialize in making certain small, necessary things like soap and candles. Of course, we were able to make all of them, too, but it was easier to let others specialize in making one thing. It also helped them out for us to trade things like meat and grain for their products, especially those in town who didn't have all the resources we had.

Candee Smith was already skilled at making candles and she was able to "hire" several of her friends to help her since the demand for candles was so high now. Mr. and Mrs. Turrow, who lived just outside of town, got good at making soap because they had two large cast iron pots needed to render the fat and mix it with the wood ash lye. They, too, were able to hire workers to help make the soft soap they traded to others. To make hard bars of soap, you have to add salt, which was in short supply in the first year after PF2 Day, so we made do with soft soap poured into whatever container we had in our possession. We used this soap for everything from washing our clothes and dishes to washing our bodies. It worked like a charm, and we were amazed that one product could so easily replace the dozens of products we used before PF Day.

Again, the town had set up a trading center in the town square when the weather was decent and moved into the school gym when it wasn't. Mom and Robin started trading their dried herbs in town almost every week. They became experts in medicinal uses for herbs and, along with Mrs. Littleton, were able to grow and sell plants from their greenhouses well into January.

Almost every time we came to town, someone would have a problem that they needed Mom and Robin's help with. They were usually able to help with minor problems like sprained ankles or sore throats or stomachaches, but a mother once came to them for help for her little boy who had severe pain in his belly, and nothing they had in their herbal arsenal would help.

His parents had to borrow a horse and rush him to another nearby town where a doctor lived, who was able to perform an appendectomy on him to save his life. That shook Mom up, and she realized just how limited her knowledge and abilities actually were.

Tipton's Diner was open and busy almost every day. It was so nice to stop there and get a warm meal every time we came to town. Mr. Tipton had hired a couple of teens to help wait tables, whom he paid in food for themselves and their families. That freed Skylar up somewhat so she could come and visit me once a week. Her parents let her stay the night when she came in order to give us more time together. Jenny Garten usually came, too, and they would sleep in the family room in front of the fireplace. I always offered them my room, but they said they preferred to sleep by the fire.

Sometimes, I would sneak down in the middle of the night to sit with them and Skylar and I would talk until dawn and, at times, do a little more than talk. We never went past second base, I swear. That would have been disrespectful to our parents, and I wasn't willing to abuse their trust.

By April, the unusually mild winter had already turned into a warm, beautiful spring, and Robin had exciting news to share with us: she was pregnant. Mom wasn't surprised, as she had been noticing the signs for a few weeks. She estimated that the baby would be born around Christmas, and we were all incredibly excited. Mom and the grandmas immediately began work on clothes and diapers for the baby. We guys decided to make the baby a cradle and we had so much fun building it that we went ahead and made a crib, as well.

Spring is a time for babies on a farm, too, and we were knee deep in them: baby chicks, baby goats, a calf, and two foals. It was a happy time for our family.

Chapter 15

One night, in the first week of April, I awoke with a start to the sound of the dogs barking wildly. I sat up in bed, listened a little more carefully and, hearing nothing, lay back down to sleep, my eyes already closed as soon as my head hit the pillow. It is not unusual for our dogs to bark like that at a coyote or a fox, or even a deer that has wandered onto the property. The dogs were more than able to run off any predator before they could get close enough to the chickens to grab a free Happy Meal.

I was quickly falling back into a peaceful slumber when the scream of air horns blasted away any hope of sleep.

You see, Dad and Rick Thomas had rigged up a defense system all around the livestock fences and the silos. Basically, they had run an electric fence around the outside of the fences and on the ladders to the silos, which were powered by the batteries from their tractors, combines, and other machines. When the fence or ladders were touched, they not only gave an electrical shock but also activated air horns, which could be heard from over two miles away. The wire on the fence and the ladders were placed too high for the dogs or any small predators to hit them, so we knew instantly when we were dealing with something larger than a coyote or even the rare visit from a mountain lion.

I raced to my window, which faces east toward the backyard, while pulling on my jeans, boots, and a sweatshirt, and tried to see what was out there. The moon was not quite full, but still bright enough for me to make out the dogs around the base of one of our three silos. They were going absolutely insane, jumping wildly into the air to snap at a figure on the bottom rung of the ladder. It looked like a person to me, but the angle at which it was hanging left some doubt.

I could see the silhouettes of the horses and cows in their paddock, along with the mule and donkey, which were braying and kicking up their heels in a fit of rage. Mules and donkeys make great guard animals for a herd and will effectively scare off any predators or unwanted guests. We had given our other mule and donkey to the Thomas's to protect their herd.

As I raced down the stairs, I almost collided with Alex and Calvin, and we met Dad at the bottom, who was holding two rifles. Mom was next to him, clutching the shotgun and another rifle. We had another two rifles and a shotgun, which Papa and the others would use to defend the house, if necessary.

As we flew out the back door, Dad said, "Remember, we want to scare 'em off, not kill 'em." He paused and added, "But make every shot count." We were already on a limited supply of bullets, after all.

The noise outside was unbelievably loud. Besides the air horns blaring and the dogs barking, the mule and donkey were still braying madly, the horses were neighing in terror, and the chickens were squawking their indignation at being so rudely woken up. The dogs backed up to let us at the figure on the ladder, which we could now see was indeed a man hanging from his elbow, unconscious, and shuddering as the electric current still ran through him.

The ladders on our silos started about five feet off the ground, so you had to jump up to grab the first rung; this was to keep kids from climbing them. We were a little surprised that the intruder hadn't been blown off the ladder from the initial shock, but maybe his elbow had caught him up. At any rate, Dad flipped off the switch he had rigged on the battery and we pulled the guy to the ground. He was still unconscious, but starting to moan and wake up. Dad told me and Calvin to drag him up to the house for Mom to look him over, while he and Alex checked around for other intruders.

"Keep an eye on him, though," he warned. "Don't turn your back on him for a second."

About halfway to the house, the guy started twisting around wildly like a gator in a death roll, trying to get his hands free from our grasp. Mom ran out with a shotgun aimed right at him and said, in a menacing tone that both surprised me and made me proud, "You better just settle down there, young man, before I fill you full of buckshot."

The guy stopped struggling and looked at her with such a frightened expression that I almost burst out laughing. I could picture Mom in a long, old-west style skirt holding a shotgun over an unfortunate cattle rustler. My amusement didn't last long, however, because just then we heard the crack of gunfire and a strangled yell. Then men were shouting and I yelled at Calvin to stay with Mom while I ran down toward the field to see what was going on.

As I neared the field, I could see Dad standing guard over Alex, while he sat on the ground, and the dogs were about a quarter of a mile downfield, chasing three people. Ben, our Great Pyrenees/German Shepherd/who-knows-what mix, was rapidly gaining on them, when one turned around and shot him with what appeared to be a pistol. Ben whimpered and fell to the ground while the men scrambled over a fence and ran off, the other two dogs lunging at the fence that they couldn't quite clear, all the while growling and barking wildly.

I ran after them, stopping only when I reached Ben, who was whimpering softly and lying on his side. I could see a dark stain of what I assumed was blood on his shoulder as I knelt down to examine and comfort him. Calvin came running up then, and I felt a panic rising in me at the sight of him. "Mom!" was all I could get out, but Calvin quickly told me that Papa was with her and they had the guy tied up on the back porch. In the distance I could see Robin kneeling over Alex and, even at this distance, I could hear her crying.

"Is Alex okay?" I asked Calvin.

"Yeah, it just winged his ear. Lots of blood, though. How's Ben?"

"He's been shot in the shoulder, I think. Let's try to carry him back to the house."

"What about the bad guys?" asked Calvin, with a little tremor in his voice. I couldn't tell whether it was fear or adrenaline that caused him to sound like that.

"I think they're gone," I said, with more than a little doubt in my voice.

The other two dogs had stopped barking and were sniffing Ben worriedly. I petted each in turn to try to calm them down and assure them that he was going to be okay. I also wanted to let them know that they had done a good job, chasing the bad guys away.

Dad came jogging up to us and said, "Is he alright?" to which I repeated that he'd been shot in the shoulder. Dad scooped him up tenderly and began carrying him toward the house, saying, "Watch my back, boys. We don't want those assholes to sneak up on us."

Now, as I've said before, Dad is strong. That dog weighs at least 120 pounds, but Dad was carrying him like he was a little baby, cradled in his arms with his head resting on Dad's shoulder. Dad wasn't usually very demonstrative with the dogs, but they shared a quiet devotion to each other that didn't need to be advertised.

By the time we'd made it back to the house, everyone had gone inside. Mom was putting some kind of herbal antiseptic on Alex's ear – or I should say, on the notch that was taken out of the top of it. He was holding hands with Robin, who was still sniffling and leaning her head against his other shoulder. The intruder was sitting in one of the straight-backed kitchen chairs near the fire and was looking down at his hands that were tied in front of him. I looked at him curiously. He didn't look like a bad guy at all, just a scared, skinny kid about my age. I felt kind of sorry for him, even though his friends had shot my brother and my dog.

Dad laid Ben on the coffee table and sat beside him with his hand on his head to keep him calm. He glanced over at the stranger and said to Mom, "What's his story?"

Papa was the one to answer him. "He's just a kid, John. Scared and hungry. Hasn't said a word, though."

Dad thought about that for a minute, then said quietly, "Well, let's give him something to eat."

Gram smiled, and she and Granny went to the kitchen to find him some food. Gram never liked to see anybody hungry. She always said, "I lived through the Great Depression, and I've seen too many hungry people."

Gram came back carrying a huge plate of ham, home-canned green beans, and homemade bread spread thick with our butter. Granny handed him a glass of milk. At first, it appeared he wasn't going to take it. He turned his head to the side and I could see the glint of tears on his cheeks in the soft glow of the oil lamp. But the hunger must have gotten the better of him, because he tore into the plate of food with his bound hands. Gram patted his shoulder and I could see a fresh trail of tears spill onto his cheek.

After he'd finished the plateful of food and a second plateful that Gram gave him, he finally looked up at us. "I'm sorry," was all he could get out before breaking down. He buried his face in his hands while silent sobs made his shoulders quake.

Gram looked at Dad with tears in her own eyes and said, "John, don't you think we could untie him now? He doesn't seem like he's going to hurt us."

Dad gazed at Ben for a few seconds then said, dejectedly, "Yeah, I guess so."

I went over to the kid and untied the rope around his wrists. "What's your name?" I asked him. He looked up at me kind of scared but also grateful and said, "Ben."

We were all a little taken aback, what with Ben the dog lying there on the coffee table. At the mention of his name, he lifted his head weakly and tried to make his friendly "hello" bark, but it came out sounding a little drunk. I wondered if anybody had mentioned the dog's name. Maybe the kid was mocking us, but if so, he must be a great actor because he had such a sincere look on his face.

Mom finished bandaging Alex's ear, and then moved her medicines and her attention to the dog. After feeling around in the wound, during which time Ben the dog laid perfectly still, as if he knew that any movement would make it harder for Mom to fix him, Mom smiled and said, "I don't think it's too bad. It looks like the bullet just nicked him, too. Thank goodness those guys were bad shots."

Dad smiled, too. We all did, and even Ben the kid couldn't keep his lips from turning up a little at the corners.

Later that evening, after I had given Ben the kid some of my sweat pants and a shirt, since his were all torn and dirty, he started opening up to us. His name was Ben Michaels and he had come up with three other young men from Kansas City. He told us that his parents had both died during that first hard winter after PF Day. When I looked into his eyes, I could tell that he had buried the pain of the memories, but it was there, lurking right under the surface, biding its time before it consumed him. I couldn't imagine being in his shoes – homeless, an orphan, starving. Any leftover anger I'd had at him for trying to steal our hard-earned grain quickly flew out the window.

Mom must have felt the same way because she said, "Well, you can stay here, Ben. We have a house and a family and plenty of food to eat."

The tears started again in Ben's eyes and all he could do was nod his thanks.

"Come on, Ben. You can sleep in my room. I have two beds in there," I told him, and then led him up to my room. I could tell he was exhausted as he lay on probably the first bed he'd slept on in months, but he must have had a lot to get off his chest, because he talked to me for a long time, telling me the things he had lived through and witnessed in the year and a half since PF Day.

Chapter 16

Ben told me that he had been living with his divorced dad in an apartment in downtown Kansas City when the first solar superstorm struck. His mother lived in a suburb north of Kansas City. He had been out foraging some food and water about four months after PF Day when their apartment caught fire. Ben had come home to find the apartment building ablaze and his dad nowhere to be found.

His body, along with many others, was never recovered. The building had burned completely to the ground, taking parts of the adjacent buildings with it. Ben had spent the next few days trying to get to his mom's house on foot through deep snow and bitter cold.

Ben had not talked to his mother since before PF Day. In fact, he had not talked to her often since she married his stepfather two years before, as he didn't get along with his stepfather, but after PF Day, with no phone service, he had had no contact with her at all. He said he had been meaning to visit her to check on her, but since he knew that she had a husband to take care of her and his father had had no one but him, he had never gotten around to it.

When he arrived at her house, his stepfather told him that he should've come sooner – his mother had just died from a bad case of influenza that had most likely turned into pneumonia. He had missed seeing her alive by just two days.

Her body was stored in a shed out back with the lawnmower because they couldn't bury her until the ground thawed. That really creeped me out and when I mentioned it, Ben said it really upset him, too, but lots of bodies had to be stored that way until spring.

Heartbroken, he had spent just a few days at his stepfather's house before setting off in the snow again.

He wandered aimlessly for a while, finding shelter wherever he could – abandoned, burned out buildings, emergency shelters, friends' houses, even some kind strangers' houses. He could never stay in one place very long, though, because hunger forced him to leave to find food, and when he came back his place would always be taken by some other homeless person.

Somehow, he made it through the winter, and by spring had begun hanging out with several other homeless young men, all of whom were several years older than he. He had stayed with them even when the power was back on, squatting in vacant houses or buildings until someone came to kick them out. He had no home or family to go to and didn't even consider going back to school.

"What was the point anyway?" he said, and I have to admit, I understood completely. I mean, I hadn't seen the point in going back to school and I had a home and a family. And a girlfriend, of course, which was probably the only real reason I had any interest in going back at all.

Ben described the other men he hung with as just unfortunates like him; not mean guys or criminals, just desperate and hungry. Since PF2 Day, they had been working their way north toward Omaha, where one of the men had family whom he thought would take them all in, foraging and stealing on the way. At first they had begged for food and shelter, but they were run off several times by people who didn't have enough to share or enough trust to take in four wanderers. Ben said he understood their reaction – "You have to take care of your own first," he said, with little emotion in his voice. After a while, they just found it easier to steal what they could by night. That is, until they came here.

I told him I was sorry he'd gotten hurt, but he said, "No big deal. I had it comin'."

When I asked him about the gun his friend had used to shoot Alex and Ben, he said, "Funny thing is, he had just stolen that pistol from a farmhouse farther down the highway, thinking we could shoot some wild animal if we didn't find any food soon."

He explained that none of them knew anything about hunting, growing up in the city like they had, and they also knew very little about guns and shooting. I said that was no surprise and thank goodness, too, because they had almost missed their targets altogether. Ben said he was sorry about the shooting. He said he didn't know why Doug had shot at them – probably he was just freaked out at seeing his buddy (Ben) dangling from that ladder like a corpse from a noose.

Ben kept saying over and over that his buddies were not bad guys, just scared and hungry. He was determined to make me understand, and I was inclined to believe him; the horrors he was describing might drive anyone to desperation.

I asked Ben if he had any other family,

and he answered that he had grandparents and an aunt and uncle who lived in New York City. I asked him if he wanted to try to get there eventually, but he said, "Hell, no! I know how bad it is in Kansas City, and I can only imagine how much worse it'd be in New York."

He then described what life had been like for him when he was in the city. "First, there was the thirst. After the water towers ran dry and every bit of bottled or canned drink was drunk, everyone started drinking out of the creeks and fountains, but that water was pretty much tainted by sewage because the sewer system wasn't workin', and people started dyin' from horrible stomach diseases – I don't know what. If you were lucky enough to live by one of the big rivers and you had something to boil the water over, then you were probably gonna make it, but they were too far away for us.

"You'd try to set out buckets and bowls to collect rainwater, then everyone would try to steal the water you had collected and you had to stand out in the freezin' cold rain to make sure you got some. But that fall, after PF Day, it didn't rain much so most of the time you were just thirsty. We were so thirsty that we were thankful for the snow, even though we were freezin', so we could at least melt some to drink."

I had heard a little about the troubles cities had had getting water and I asked, "Didn't the army or National Guard bring in water for everyone?"

Ben laughed, but it was a hollow and sad sound. "Yeah, but it wasn't even close to enough and there were riots every time a truck came in. Everybody was so thirsty…" His voice trailed off as he remembered the ordeal. After a minute he brightened a little and said, "But it was better in the country; at least in the warmer weather, when sleeping under a tree or in somebody's shed or barn didn't freeze your junk off. At least we had water. The water in the creeks tastes good and don't make us sick. Even if it had, I'd a drunk it anyway. I'd rather die pukin' my guts out and crappin' my pants than dyin' of thirst."

Ben went on to describe all the medical problems faced by people in the city. We had some of the same problems here, but on a much smaller scale. Ben said the hospitals had become morgues since so many patients died there after the hospital generators ran out of fuel: people who were on ventilators, of course, and people who needed oxygen, or IV's, or medicines to keep them alive.

He said the saddest place in the city was the children's hospital, where hundreds of parents had to watch their children die in their arms. People started calling hospitals "black holes" because, if you were sick enough to go there, you'd probably never come back out.

After a while, doctors started making house calls, going door to door in search of people needing treatment. Sometimes the doctor would have to do emergency surgery right there in somebody's front room or on the kitchen table, but the outcome was often much better than going to the hospital, where out of control secondary diseases would kill you even if you survived the surgery.

Ben then described the hunger. He said it was not nearly as bad as the thirst; in fact, he had kind of gotten used to being hungry. "Bein' hungry ain't that bad," he said. "You just have to do somethin' to get your mind off it."

I couldn't imagine being hungry; or thirsty either, for that matter. I realized just how lucky I was to be living right where I was. According to Ben, people had gotten so hungry that they were eating stray dogs and cats, catching birds and squirrels, even mice and rats to eat. After the President had ordered the big grain elevators opened and the grain distributed, people had to figure out how to grind it up so it could be eaten, often without even being cooked. Ben said his dad had used the marble bottom of one of his bowling trophies against a small slab of concrete to grind up the corn and wheat kernels so they could be digested.

"A little pigeon rolled in cornmeal tastes pretty good when you're hungry," he said, only half joking.

Before we went to sleep, Ben asked me what the date was. When I told him it was April 8th, he smiled – a real smile this time, even though it was still kind of sad – and said that his 16th birthday was in five days. I told him we could have a birthday party for him, and we could get in the car and I could teach him to drive, even though we couldn't actually go anywhere. He smiled again and said he'd like that.

Chapter 17

When I woke up the next morning, I stretched and looked over at the bed next to me to see if Ben was stirring. All that I saw was a nicely made bed and, startled, I wondered for a second if I'd dreamed the whole thing the night before. Then, I heard the back door shut. I pulled on my boots and ran after him. He wasn't hard to catch up with and, when I did, I reached out and grabbed him by the shoulder.

"Hey, where're you going?" I asked him when he turned around.

"Just goin'," he replied.

"But why? You can stay, you know." When he didn't answer, I added, "Don't you want someplace to live?"

"Yeah, more than anything, but you guys don't need someone else to feed. You don't owe me anything."

"It's not about owing anybody anything," I answered, a little perturbed. "You need a place to live and we got a place. We got enough to eat and to feed you, too."

He looked warily at me before he said, a little suspiciously, "Why? What's in it for you?"

"I don't know," I snapped. "Why does there have to be something in it for me? Why can't we just be nice people wanting to help someone out?"

"I don't need any…" he started to say, then stopped and sighed. "I don't get it. I tried to steal from you and my friend tried to shoot your brother and your dog…"

"He did shoot them," I interrupted.

Ben looked sheepish. "Yeah, well, why would you and your parents want to help me out after all that?"

"Because you need help," I said. "Hell, you're just a kid. Those other guys are men. They can take care of themselves, but you…"

"I can take care of myself!"

"Yeah, now, while the weather's nice, but what about next winter? What're you going to do then, tough guy?" I know I was taunting him a little, but I was worried about him. I felt like he was my kid brother, like Calvin, and I didn't want to think about Calvin being out there, homeless and starving with no one offering him a place to stay.

He started to get defensive, started to tell me to go to hell or something, but then he just shrugged his shoulders and started to cry. This time he cried out loud, and my heart broke for him. I put my arms around him and let him cry into the shoulder of my sweatshirt for several minutes until it seemed he had no more tears left in him.

"It's okay, man," I said, trying to be as comforting as I could. "It's okay. We really want you to stay here."

He just nodded and we started back toward the house. By the time we went inside, Mom was up and starting breakfast. She didn't glance at us as we went back upstairs, so I could get dressed and Ben could compose himself. I had the feeling that she had seen us out the window and didn't want to embarrass him.

At breakfast, Ben timidly asked Dad if he thought that any of the guys he was with were shot when they ran off, saying, "I just don't want 'em out there bleedin' to death with no one to help 'em. They're really not bad guys. They helped me a lot, took care of me after my parents died."

Dad answered, a little perturbed, "Well, they ran off and left you hanging there. But don't worry, we shot over their heads. We didn't want to hurt 'em, just scare 'em off. Alex and I'll go down there and check around later just to be sure." Then he added, just to remind Ben who actually got hurt, "*If* he's up to it."

Later that day, Skylar and Jenny came to visit. I ran out to meet them as soon as I heard the clip-clop of their horses' hooves on the pavement of the highway. It scared me to think they had ridden over here with those marauders on the loose, but hopefully they were long gone by now. I was kissing Skylar hello when Ben and Calvin walked up to us. I purposely held on to the kiss just a little longer than normal to show Ben she belonged to me, just in case he got any ideas.

Jenny jumped down and said hello before looking to me with raised eyebrows as if to say, "C'mon, introduce him, will you?"

"This is Ben," I said casually. "He's going to be staying with us for a while." Ben looked at me a little gratefully, probably since I didn't mention just how he came to be with us.

Jenny walked over to him and stuck out her hand to shake, saying, "It's nice to meet you, Ben. Are you going riding with us?" I could tell she was very interested in him. Her voice sounded different – flirtatious, I guess.

Ben returned the interest, but replied, "I don't know how to ride a horse."

Jenny giggled – actually giggled – and said, "That's okay. You can ride with me." Ben eagerly agreed.

Calvin didn't seem too happy about Ben taking over his usual spot and said, "I can saddle up Big Red for him. He's gentle enough for a baby to ride."

"Oh, Calvin, *you* can ride Big Red," Jenny replied condescendingly. "Let the guest choose."

Of course, Ben chose to ride with Jenny. Calvin suddenly decided he had something else to do and went back in the house with a scowl on his face. I felt kind of bad for him. After all, he and Jenny had had a thing going for a while and now he was being thrown out like yesterday's trash. I felt sorry for him, but not enough to go after him.

We rode around our land, keeping an eye out for the bad guys, which Ben kept reminding us were not really bad guys. We eventually told the girls the whole story of what had happened the night before, and they listened with a sort of cautious wonder. After all, not many exciting things happened in Holt County, either before or since PF Day.

Skylar turned halfway around in the saddle so she could hug me tight, saying,

"Now, I won't be able to sleep, worrying about you." I knew she was overreacting, but I enjoyed her concern anyway. I glanced at Ben because I felt his eyes on us and was a little pissed off to see him staring longingly at Skylar. He quickly looked away when he noticed my glare.

All day long, I kept catching him looking at Skylar and laughing a little too loudly at her jokes and maneuvering himself to stand closer to her anytime he could. Skylar seemed not to notice, but Jenny did, and I could see the jealousy growing with every little bit of attention Ben showed Skylar. I could tell I was going to have to have a serious talk with that boy later on that night.

Dad and Alex had taken a couple of the horses and ridden the perimeter of the farm, looking for traces of Ben's friends and, finding none, they rode over to check on the Thomas's and the other neighbors, like Mr. and Mrs. Caruthers and Johnny and Crystal Phillips. Nobody had seen any men, but Johnny said one of his chickens was missing. That in itself didn't prove anything, but Dad told everyone to be careful anyway. "Better to let 'em take a few chickens than to risk being shot at," he told them.

We were out riding all afternoon and

came back for dinner around sunset. After brushing the horses down and putting them in the paddock, we went inside. I made sure to seat Skylar between Robin and me at dinner so Ben couldn't sit by her. Instead, he took a seat directly across from her and, even though Jenny sat next to him, he spent more time looking at Skylar. Skylar tried to ignore him for the most part and kept turning to me to whisper silly things in my ear, which kept us both giggling at the table. At one point, Mom gave me a look that reminded me it was not polite to whisper, so we just held hands under the table and gazed at each other. I thought that would send Ben a clear message.

Either he hadn't been paying attention to my message or he didn't care, because later that night, after we had all gone to sleep, I woke up in the middle of the night and Ben was gone. *Great*, I thought. I started down the stairs quietly and met Skylar halfway, tiptoeing up to get me.

"Can you put your friend on a leash?" she whispered with a meaningful grin on her face. I thought about taking Skylar up to my room instead of back down to the living room, but I wasn't sure if Ben could be trusted alone with Jenny, so I reluctantly led

Skylar back down.

Ben was sitting near Jenny, but his eyes lit up when he saw Skylar and he said, "You're back!" just a little too enthusiastically for my taste. Jenny's too, apparently, because she hauled off and punched him in the shoulder.

He looked at her all innocent-like and said, "What was that for?" She just shook her head and turned away from him.

After we settled down and talked for an hour or so, the girls said they wanted to go to sleep, so Ben and I went back to my room. I told him that Skylar was my girlfriend and we were probably going to get married someday, so he'd better back off. He just shrugged his shoulders and said, "Whatever, man. I didn't mean anything by it. Just bein' friendly."

"A little too friendly," I grumbled, to which he turned his back on me. I wasn't very happy with the outcome of the conversation, and I still didn't trust him. I knew I'd have to keep my eye on Ben, and I didn't sleep well at all that night.

Chapter 18

The girls went home the next day. To my satisfaction – and Jenny's delight – Ben paid little attention to Skylar and focused most of his interest on Jenny. Still, I didn't quite trust him, so when I rode to town later in the week to visit Skylar, I promised Calvin I'd do his chores for a week if he found some way to keep Ben occupied at home. Mom wasn't too keen on me riding alone, so Dad volunteered to go with me, saying he had some business in town to take care of anyway.

We took the wagon, which Dad loaded up with some buckets of grain and tubs of homemade butter to trade. With two milk cows, our family had more than enough milk and butter, so we could afford to sell off some of our supply. Since we couldn't keep the milk cold for long, we usually ended up giving a lot of it to the dogs and the barn cats, but the butter kept longer without refrigeration and we had plenty to spare.

Dad was making plans to repurpose the old storm cellar out back into a cold cellar, but the past winter had been too mild to collect enough ice to line it with. Still, it was cooler than the outside air, and we had been storing our smoked meats, along with some apples, carrots, onions, and potatoes in there for use in the warmer weather.

I had a great time in town with Skylar, as always, and Dad was able to trade his wares for lumber to make shelves for the cold cellar.

The next day, we got right to work on building shelves and, although Ben tried to help, he really didn't know anything about using tools or making things. It took twice as long, because we kept having to stop and show him how to do something; nonetheless, Dad said it was important that he learned how to do things right.

The idea behind a cold cellar started way back in olden days, before there was any kind of electricity or anything else to keep things cold. It's basically a hole in the ground, fortified so it doesn't cave in, although if you're lucky enough to have a natural cave on your property, it saves you a lot of work. The hole has to be several feet underground so that the food is kept at a constant 50° all year. Dad had us dig another, smaller room at the back of the original storm shelter, with its own thick, insulated door to keep food even colder. If you cut blocks of ice from a frozen pond or, like Dad planned to do, set water out in buckets on below-freezing days, then put the ice in the "freezer" room and cover them with straw, they will stay mostly frozen through the summer, keeping whatever is stored in with them frozen, as well.

Another alternative that Dad thought about was using our electric deep freeze and burying it in the ground, but he decided that once you added the blocks of ice inside of it, you wouldn't have enough room for much food. Instead, he just used the door of the freezer as the door to the new freezer room, and the shelves of the freezer to store food on.

Dad decided that we needed to expand the storm cellar, so we spent several days digging it deeper into the ground. Ben complained to me the entire time when Dad wasn't around to hear it and he'd lean on his shovel to take a break whenever he could, but when Dad showed up again, he looked busy and eager to work. When I mentioned his behavior to Dad, he said, "Don't worry, I know his kind. He'll either get used to working like us, or he'll get tired of it and leave." I have to hand it to my Dad; he's a shrewd man.

Mom is a shrewd woman, too. Ben was always giving her compliments and rushing over to help her carry something light up the stairs, but was curiously absent when she needed someone to do the hard work. Mom noticed right away and, after a couple of days of this, she pulled him aside and had a talk with him.

I know I shouldn't have, but I eavesdropped on the conversation. She told him, nicely, that actions speak louder than words – something she always said – and that a real compliment to her would be for him to offer to take some of the tougher jobs off her hands, like filling and dumping the washing machine tub or wringing the clothes out. In fact, she added, if he really wanted to show his appreciation, he could take over the laundry altogether. I had to stifle my laughter at her cleverness.

We were out checking the fence line one day, about two weeks after Ben started staying with us. Ben, Calvin, and I had gone one direction while Dad and Alex had gone in the opposite direction, and we were supposed to fix any wire or post that was down. At one point, Ben went off behind some trees to relieve himself and never came back. When I went to check on him and tell him to hurry up, he quickly stumbled out from behind a big clump of bushes and said, "C'mon, we're wasting daylight."

I could have gotten on to him about how *he* was the one wasting time, that he always liked to waste time; I just shook my head and went back to checking the fence.

That night, after we had been asleep for several hours, I woke up to the sound of the back door shutting and the dogs barking. I noticed that Ben's bed was made up, and he wasn't in it. Déjà vu.

When I looked out my window, I saw Ben petting the dogs to settle them down, and then walking away with three men. I remembered the strange way he had acted earlier that day. He must have been talking to his friends in the bushes during his ridiculously long bathroom break. They had come back for him. Maybe he was right – they weren't so bad after all if they cared enough to come back for him.

I went downstairs and found Dad watching them from the kitchen window. I asked him if we should go after him, but he said, "No, he's gotta make his own choices," and I knew he was referring to the choice of whether to work hard or leave.

Dad told me that Ben had taken a loaf of

bread and some ham, but that was okay. He would have given the kid more if he'd asked. I have to say, this time I wasn't sad to see him go, but I did hope he would be all right. I mean, I liked the guy and all; he was just kind of a pain in the butt. I guess he wasn't so different than any of us brothers, when I got to thinking about it. Unlike my brothers, however, I didn't share a history with Ben, so I was more willing to let him go than if it had been Alex or Calvin. Well, maybe just Calvin.

Jenny was the one who I thought would be really upset to see him go, but the next time she and Skylar visited, she didn't act surprised at all when she found out that he wasn't there. I thought that was odd until she let slip that Ben was living in town with the other three men, in a house whose owner had died last winter.

Great, I thought – now he'd be able to see Skylar more than I could.

Jenny made me feel better by saying that she and Ben were dating now, and that he and his friends were doing odd jobs around town for the necessities of life. She said his friends seemed nice enough, although they weren't very motivated. Apparently, they worked only enough to get some food, and then they would just leave and go home. They were allowed to live in the house for free because no one owned it, or at least no one that anyone knew about.

The old woman who had lived there had children, but they lived elsewhere and hadn't come to claim the house yet. The town police officer told them that they could live there, as long as they took care of the place, until the rightful owners came to tell them otherwise.

My family thought we had gotten off easy – concerning marauders, that is. To hear the Guardsmen talk, the marauders would have killed us all at the drop of a hat. I was feeling pretty safe right then, and I said so one night at dinner, but Papa said, "Calm always comes before the storm," to which Dad replied, "Some days you get the bear, other days the bear gets you." Then Calvin said, in his best Forrest Gump voice, "Life is like a box of chocolates…"

We all busted up laughing, but, later, I thought about what Dad and Papa had said and I started worrying again.

What if Ben and his friends weren't rep-resentative of most marauders? What if some would show up and really hurt us? Even worse, what if they went into town and hurt Skylar and I wasn't there to defend her?

Not being able to sleep at night was beginning to become a habit with me, and I didn't care too much for it.

Chapter 19

That summer was great – one of the happiest I could remember. After the spring planting – which was kind of hard until we got the hang of the horse-drawn planter Dad had gotten from Mr. Caruthers – I was pretty much free to do about anything I wanted after all my chores were done for the day.

Skylar got a job with Johnny and Crystal Phillips watching their two little girls while they worked around their farm. The Phillips's live just a little over four miles from our house, and Skylar stayed with them during the week. The Phillips's didn't mind if I came and hung out with Skylar just as long as I helped her with the girls. I often assisted Johnny with work that was harder for Crystal, although she was pretty strong for such a little gal.

On the weekends, Skylar came and stayed with my family at our house. I wondered if her parents missed her a lot, and she said that they were pretending she was just away at summer camp or something. Sometimes she would get homesick, and we would ride to town and stay with her parents for the weekend. I slept on the couch in their family room and minded my manners, as my Mom brought me up to do.

I always helped Mr. and Mrs. Tipton with whatever they needed help with, and I could tell that they really liked me. Mr. Tipton even started calling me "son" and told me to call him Dave. Try as I might, though, it was really hard to shake the habit of calling him Mr. Tipton and it took all summer before I felt comfortable with it.

Mrs. Tipton wanted me to call her Barb, too, and that was just a little easier because I was more familiar with her. Skylar had felt so comfortable from the beginning calling my Mom and Dad by their given names. I guess that's because she had waited on them so often in the diner and felt like they were old friends. Or maybe it was just Skylar – she's so comfortable being herself ever since she was liberated from the diner.

One day in June, Ben came riding to our house with Jenny. It was a Saturday, so Skylar was already at our house and we all spent the day riding around and having a good time. I liked Ben much more since he wasn't interested in Skylar anymore and I have to give it to him, he had respected my warning about her right away. However, there was still one thing that bothered me about him.

He kept talking about how he and his buddies had been working on making explosive devices, and they wanted to make up for the trouble they had caused our family by helping us set up a better defense system for marauders. I wasn't sure exactly what their intentions were and it made me a little uneasy.

Ben told Dad later about the idea and Dad was a little skeptical, too, but agreed to hear them out. It was decided that Ben would bring his friends back in a couple of days to talk to Dad and show him what they had come up with. After Ben and Jenny had left that afternoon, Dad said we would have to be ready for any shenanigans they might pull. He wanted to believe that their intentions were true, but he said, "You can never be too careful."

Two days later, true to his word, Ben came back with his three buddies. They had borrowed Jenny's two horses and were riding double on them, each with a backpack full of stuff. As Ben introduced his friends, the one named Doug was very sheepish and apologetic. He was the one who had shot at Alex and Ben the dog. He said he had panicked when he thought that Ben had been killed, but that he regretted even having the gun in the first place, especially when Ben the kid told them how kind we had been to him. He seemed sincere, and Alex and Dad both assured him that he was forgiven.

The men explained to us that they had started a sort of business to help people protect themselves against marauders. Since they had been forced to steal themselves for a while, they knew that the probability of vandalism and attacks would only get worse as people became more desperate and more dangerous with the coming winter. Doug explained that they were trading their expertise for food and other necessities, but that they had all agreed to give free help to us for the trouble they had caused.

Papa pulled Dad aside and whispered that they may just be trying to set us up to steal from us, but Dad said he'd already thought of that, and he had some tricks up his sleeve in case that was their ulterior motive.

So, we all gathered around the guys and listened as they described how to make homemade grenades, torpedoes, and tear gas out of common household items. Dad asked them how they knew so much about making homemade weapons and one of the guys, Matt, said that he had been a zombie movie fan and had a book about what to do in the event of a zombie apocalypse. We all laughed, but he mentioned how the part about making homemade weapons was real, and he and the others had tried them out. They helped us make several different types of weapons and gave us pointers on how to protect ourselves and our property from zombies (or any other type of invader).

The guys also told us that we should keep some food in a box near the highway, off the ground and secure from animals, like our mailbox, with a sign that offered it to travelers. This way, hungry people just trying to get someplace, like the four of them had been, could get food without having to steal or beg from us.

We agreed that it was a good idea and decided to make a larger box to contain enough food to get a group of travelers a few miles. If that amount of food didn't satisfy those who came for it, then they were probably up to no good anyway.

When we took a break to have lunch, which Mom and the grandmas insisted the guys eat, too, I got to talking with Dakota, the third man, about who they were and how they had met. Dakota told me that the three of them had been engineering majors at UMKC and had shared a dorm. Shortly after

PF Day, the university kicked everyone out of the dorms because they had to shut the whole campus down. The guys didn't have a way to get back home to their families, each of whom lived quite a distance away, so they hung out together in Kansas City, seeking shelter and scavenging food wherever they could find it.

They had found Ben, nearly frozen and starving to death, and had taken him under their wing. They had been planning to try to make it to Omaha, which was the closest city where any of them had relatives, when they found an opportunity to live in our town. The townspeople had been so friendly and helpful to them that they had decided to stay, at least until they found a better way to get to Omaha than walking.

After talking to Dakota, I felt much better about the three of them as people, and so did the rest of my family when I told them their story later that night.

Dad, Alex, and Papa decided that it couldn't hurt to fix up some of the weapons the guys had told us about, so we spent several days working out all sorts of scenarios and provisioning the farm with defense systems. We had quite a lot of fun talking about zombies and started calling any type of marauder that might threaten us "zombies."

We even taught Mom, Robin, and the grandmas how to use the various weapons in all the places we had set them up, and we went over emergency plans in case of "zombie" attacks. Even though we were enjoying ourselves – it was kind of like setting up to play a video game or to be in a zombie movie or something – there was always a sense of seriousness and real concern in our actions. We all knew that being a lone farm right off the highway, with plenty of grain and livestock, put us in danger just like the National Guardsmen had warned us about.

Our neighbors, the Thomas's, were in danger, too, so Dad and Alex went to their house and helped them. The Fab Four, as we had begun calling Ben and his buddies, had already been there, so Alex and Dad had only to help the couple implement what they had been taught. One of the things that the Fab Four had enthusiastically approved of was the air horns. They believed that if a gang of marauders was scared off from one farm, they would probably go to the next one to see if they would have better luck, so advanced warning like that could make a big difference.

It was also agreed upon that if we heard

the alarm go off at the Thomas's', two of us would ride over to see if they needed help, but since there were only the two of them, they could not return the favor. Rick Thomas felt really bad about that, but Dad convinced him that he couldn't leave his place unguarded to come to our aid, nor could he leave his wife, Carla, at home to defend it herself.

Mom felt uneasy about me going to the Phillips's alone to see Skylar, without anything to defend myself, so I started taking my shotgun with me. We had fashioned gun scabbards for the saddles and I felt like a regular cowboy with my gun on my saddle and my hunting knife in my boot. I hoped I would never have to use either of them, but they made Mom feel better about me going places alone.

All this talk of zombies and marauders made it hard for me to sleep at night, in spite of the defense systems we had in place. I would lay awake for nights, thinking I'd heard a noise in the yard, or going over scenarios and plans in my mind so I could execute my part flawlessly when the time came. I knew that was probably impossible, since there was no way to cover every scenario, but it made me feel better anyway.

Chapter 20

I couldn't believe how fast the summer went by; in the blink of an eye, it was already fall. Although Skylar was still helping the Phillips's while they harvested their huge vegetable garden, Crystal canned dozens of jars of vegetables, and Johnny got their small herd of cattle ready for winter, I wasn't able to spend as much time with her as I had during the summer. We had harvesting and preparing for winter going on at our house, too.

We had about 200 acres of grain to harvest, hay to cut and bale, logs to chop for the fire, and our own large garden to harvest. Mom, Robin, and the grandmas canned over a hundred jars of fruit and vegetables and always needed help carrying them down to the cold cellar. We also "laid in" potatoes, carrots, onions, apples, sweet potatoes, turnips, radishes, and several varieties of herbs in the cold cellar.

That Thanksgiving was enjoyable, as usual. Skylar got to spend the day with us and we were all able to take a much-needed break from all the winter preparations. We had plenty of food, the weather was warm, and all of our family was happy and healthy.

The weather waited until early December to get cooler, and that is when the live-stock owners did their butchering. Calvin and I helped the Phillips's and Dad and Alex helped the Thomas's. We each earned a side of beef for our help, so we traded two sides of beef for two sides of hog from the Smithson's. We spent the first two weeks of December butchering, smoking, rendering fat, boiling bones and hooves for glue, etc. By the middle of December, we felt we could finally sit back, relax, and enjoy the holidays.

Well, except for the upcoming birth of Robin's baby. Mom and the grandmas were still making clothing for the baby and diapers stuffed with absorbent down feathers.

Now, normally I don't keep track of the date. Mom keeps a calendar in the kitchen where she marks off each day, but I don't really need to know most of the time. One date will forever stick out in my mind, however, because of all the things that happened on that particular day – December 17th.

I was woken out of a deep sleep by the barking of the dogs sometime before dawn. As I strained to hear any unusual noises, my ears picked up the faint sound of an air horn coming from the direction of the Thomas's' farm. I jumped out of bed, pulled on my clothes, and met Dad, Mom, Calvin, and Alex in the kitchen. As per our plan, Dad and Calvin prepared to ride to the Thomas's' while the rest of us prepared to defend our farm. I felt a shot of adrenaline running through my veins and was surprised to find that, instead of being afraid as I thought I would be, I was actually excited. I know, kind of a dumb response, but I couldn't help it; I was psyched.

Dad and Calvin rode off at a gallop with their rifles in the saddle scabbards and pistols in their coat pockets. Alex hesitated before following me outside and I heard him tell Mom to check on Robin, who hadn't been feeling good all night. He and I then saddled our horses and began to patrol our land, careful never to stray too far from the house.

After what seemed like hours, but was probably only fifteen or twenty minutes, we heard gunfire from the Thomas's' farm. You would not believe how hard it was to stay where we were when we heard that. We had no way of knowing if Dad and Calvin were the ones shooting or if they were the ones getting shot at. We wanted so badly to gallop over and help, but we couldn't leave Mom and the others without our protection. Alex would not leave Robin, due to give birth any day. I really understood the phrase "between a rock and a hard place" at that moment.

After a few more minutes, we heard shouting and the sound of people running on the highway. The setting moon was about three-quarters full, and soon we could see a bunch of men coming toward us. Alex told me not to shoot until we were sure they were bad guys. I was still trying to figure out how I was going to know when the group suddenly spread out and began to surround the front of our property. There must have been at least thirty or forty of them and they were swarming us from all sides before we could decide who to shoot first.

I need to take a time-out here to tell you how our property is laid out, so you will be able to understand how difficult it was for Alex and me to defend it against that many people. Our house faces west, toward the highway, and sits about a hundred yards back from it. A gravel driveway goes past the house and back to the barn, which sits another hundred yards behind the house. On the north side of the barn sits the three grain silos and the paddock extends to the east of the barn and silos for about twenty acres.

Beyond that are woods. On both sides of our house, extending out for several hundred yards in both directions, are parts of our fields, surrounded on both sides by more woods. We have creeks running here and there through the woods, so we always have water to replenish our well. Across the highway to the east of our property is more woodland extending for a couple of miles. These woods are owned by a man from out of town who used to use it to hunt on once a year.

Now, back to the early morning of December 17th. The sun was beginning to rise behind us and I could just make out the faces of our opposition. They were all yelling and screaming so loud that I couldn't hear what Alex was saying. Our horses were scared and prancing wildly and I was afraid I might lose control of mine. I knew I couldn't pull my gun out and shoot at anything and still stay on the horse.

Apparently, Alex thought the same, because he motioned for me to fall back to the house, where we dismounted, let the horses go, and prepared to shoot at the crazy horde flooding into our front yard.

These were definitely not zombies! In fact, I never understood how zombies could take over the world anyway. I mean, they're so slow moving and they have no weapons. These guys seemed to be flying at us with their blood-curdling screams and their hands in the air, and now we could see that most of them held some kind of weapon in their hands, not guns, but something to throw or hit with. I had the distinct impression of the Indians in a cowboy movie and, as they got closer and closer, I half expected to see war paint on their faces.

I kept hearing that old song by Trapt, *Headstrong*, playing over and over in my mind: "Back off, I'll take you on, headstrong to take on anyone, I know that you are wrong, and this is not where you belong." I got off a couple of rounds and one guy fell about thirty yards in front of the porch. Another guy threw something at me, but I was able to duck as it sailed over my head and slammed into the wall of the house. I could hear other objects hitting the walls and even breaking windows. Alex shot a couple of people too, and that seemed to change the direction of the horde. Instead of advancing toward us, they now started circling around both sides of the house.

From Calvin's room on the second floor, the one that faced south, came one of our homemade grenades, followed by one from the opposite side of the house. I could hear Mom and Papa shooting at them from both sides of the back porch. Gram and Granny were tossing the grenades out the upstairs windows and, after only three or four of them, the marauders started backing off.

Several had been shot or injured and lay on the grass, moaning or still and silent. I don't know how many shots I had fired, but my shotgun only holds six, so I knew I'd need to reload soon. Alex motioned for us to go into the house, so we backed in through the front door and took up our positions at the living room windows while we reloaded.

Mom and Papa also came in the back door and we set ourselves up like soldiers defending our fort. Papa had blood dripping from the side of his head where he'd apparently been hit with something, but he assured us he was all right, that it would take more than a rock to keep him down. He waved off Mom's attempt to look at it.

It was completely silent for a few moments. The intruders had stopped shouting and we had stopped shooting and throwing grenades. Then, the dogs began growling and I realized, to my sudden relief, that someone had brought them into the house. All of a sudden, an air horn began screaming, and I could hear the mule and the donkey braying like they were possessed, the horses neighing, and hooves pounding the ground as they ran off down the paddock.

A few minutes later, the other air horn started blaring and the noise was almost unbearable. I thought I heard someone screaming. First it sounded like a man's voice; then I thought it was a woman's. The dogs were barking wildly again, and I thought my head was going to explode.

Mom and Papa had started firing their guns out the back windows. I couldn't see any more intruders in the front yard, and Alex shouted at me to help Mom and Papa in back. I ran to the dining room on the southeast side of the house and opened the window. A few men were crouching in the bushes along the driveway and I shot at them, wounding at least two. They yelped and all of them started running toward the highway. Gram or Granny threw another grenade, this time out my window facing the backyard and I heard another scream over the blare of the air horns, which were beginning to wane in volume.

Papa shouted, "They're on the run now! Let's chase 'em off!" I don't remember ever hearing Papa so excited.

I went back to the living room and Alex and I went out on the front porch, while Mom and Papa went out the back door. I knew we were getting low on ammunition, so I saved my bullets, shouting at them instead, using words that I would never be allowed to use under normal circumstances. I figured I'd apologize to Mom and the grandmas later.

The intruders were running north, in the opposite direction from the Thomas's'. I heard the sound of hooves coming from the south and soon saw Dad and Calvin galloping over the hill toward the fleeing men. Alex and I ran to the barn to look for our horses and found them cowering in a stall. We coaxed them out, jumped on them, and joined Dad and Calvin in the chase.

We slowed our mounts to a trot when we got near the men; we wanted to run them off, not confront them. From behind, I counted thirty-two of them. I couldn't believe so many people would band together like that to cause mayhem. I guess, like the Guardsman had said, desperate times called for desperate measures.

After we had run them several miles up the highway, some scattering off into the woods as we went, the remaining two dozen or so were exhausted and dropping like flies. We didn't know what to do with them then. None of us had ever dreamed of that many marauders showing up at our farm, and we didn't have a plan for what to do with them once we fought them off. We slowed the horses to a stop and just stood there looking at them.

One of the guys turned around and started running straight at Dad's horse, screaming like a banshee and with a look of crazed fierceness in his eyes. Dad yelled for him to stop, but nothing fazed him; he just kept coming, an axe raised over his head.

Dad had no choice but to shoot him. I could tell Dad didn't want to do it. Hell, none of us did, but like I said, he had no choice.

After that, the remaining men just sat or lay down in the road in surrender. Some were injured with gunshot or shrapnel wounds, some with burns from the grenades. We backed our horses up until we were about forty yards away from them so we could talk about what to do next. I mean, we didn't want to just let these guys go to start terrorizing our neighbors. We couldn't very well run them all to town, either. Our jail only has two cells and, even if you stuffed three or four of them in each cell, that didn't even come close to holding them all.

Alex half-jokingly suggested we should just shoot them all, but none of us really wanted to gun down now-defenseless men.

We were sitting there on the horses, letting them rest and discussing what to do, when over the hill came several of our neighbors on horseback, led by Rick Thomas. Rick told us that they had come to help, and the other men left their horses by us, walking to the bad guys and tying their hands before tying all of them together like a chain gang. Again, it looked just like a scene out of an old Western until Donald Banks and his son David, who was a year ahead of me in school, rode up in their wagon made from the bed, axles, and wheels of an old pickup truck and pulled by two horses. That was just a little too surreal for me, and I had to blink twice to bring my brain back to modern times.

In the back of the pickup-wagon sat five wounded men, the worst of them with bandages covering their wounds, and down the middle of the pickup bed lay one dead guy, half covered up. I had seen dead people before, at funerals and such, but never one that I may have killed; I had to look away and pretend everything was cool.

I was kind of relieved when Donald said, "You guys better get back home and tend to your family. Alex, your mom told me to tell you to get back right away 'cause your wife needs you."

Alex took one look at Dad and kicked his horse into a gallop toward home. Dad nodded at Donald and said, "Thanks, we'll do that."

First though, he asked Rick what they planned to do with the bad guys. Rick said that they had decided to tie them up and take them into town, where the county sheriff could hold them while Doug Arnold called the highway patrol or the National Guard over his short-wave radio. He figured they would have to be kept in the school or something until someone came for them.

Dad then told them all goodbye and thanks, and signaled for Calvin and me to follow him. I took one last look at the sorry gang of would-be zombies and kicked my horse into a trot. Suddenly, the adrenaline that had floated me along through this adventure left my system, and I was exhausted.

I slumped over my saddle horn and day-
dreamed of my bed back home all the way
there.

Chapter 21

When we got to our house, I didn't even have to tell my horse to head to the barn. Tired as we all were, we first had to unsaddle and rub down the horses, give them some hay and put them in their stalls to cool down. Calvin and I took care of Alex's horse, too, as he was understandably in a hurry to see Robin.

By the time we made it into the house roughly fifteen minutes later, Mom and my grandmas had already bandaged Papa's head, duct-taped pieces of cardboard over the broken windows, and cleaned up all the glass. Dad wanted Calvin and me to go with him to check the farm for damage, so my hopes for reuniting with my pillow were crushed.

When asked how Robin was, Mom answered, "Not too good. She may be in labor." She shook her head and added, "It looks like it's going to be a hard one."

"Anything we can do to help?" Dad asked.

"Just go do your thing and I'll call you if we need anything," she told him.

We went out and walked all over the

property, checking every detail. It looked just like you'd imagine a battlefield, with burned places here and there, splatters of blood in the grass or on the gravel of the driveway, pieces of bloody clothing, an occasional weapon dropped in haste or thrown at the house, trampled grass and broken tree branches. But the only real damage, besides the broken windows and some damage to the siding of the house, was a part of the paddock fence wire that was down, apparently cut in an attempt to get at our horses.

Luckily, the mule and/or the donkey scared them off, and the horses and cows were too spooked to try to escape the paddock later. It took only a few minutes to fix the fence, and Dad said we could clean up the rest the next day. It looked like my pillow and I were going to be reunited at last.

As soon as we got to the porch, however, I could tell that wasn't going to happen anytime soon. We could hear Robin's moans and stifled screams even through the closed windows and doors of the house. I suddenly remembered hearing a woman's scream during the battle earlier and wondered if it had been Robin.

The sound bothered all of us. We knew Robin was no crybaby. Beside Mom, she's the toughest girl I know. Hearing her in pain like that almost made me want to cry, and I think it must have affected Dad and Calvin the same way, because we all felt that cleaning up the yard was suddenly the best idea in the world.

By now it was well past lunchtime and I began to feel hungry, but I didn't want to go in and bother anyone in the house. Gram and Granny soon called us to the back porch and brought us sandwiches and hot coffee. Granny told me after we'd eaten that Robin had been asking for me. I thought I should be flattered that she would want me, out of our whole family, at her side but honestly, it just gave me butterflies. I went in anyway and crept up to her room, hearing her weak moans all the way. I wasn't prepared for the sight of her.

The poor girl lay flat on her back on the bed with her belly sticking up so high in the middle that it hid her face when I first walked in. Her face was pale and covered in sweat, her eyes dull and filled with pain. Still, she managed a little smile at me and whispered for me to sit by Alex, who was kneeling beside her head, holding her hand, stroking her hair, and occasionally wiping her face with a damp cloth. He looked almost as bad as she did. There were tears in his eyes and I could tell he would have given anything to trade places with her.

She reached over with her other hand and grabbed mine. Her hand felt hot and cold and clammy at the same time. Between gasps and moans, she was able to say to me, "Don't be scared, Bracken. It'll be alright."

Imagine that: her lying there, looking like she was at death's door, and reassuring *me*. Like I said before, you just can't help but love Robin. At that moment I was willing to take the pain for her just like Alex.

She spoke again, "When Skylar comes, tell her not to be afraid either, okay?"

I don't know where she got the idea that Skylar would be coming. She wasn't due for another couple of days. But, sure enough, she showed up later that afternoon, riding double on Rick Thomas' horse on his way back from town. I guess it must have been women's intuition that told Robin Skylar would come; maybe it was some kind of unwritten rule between women that they helped each other at a time like this. In any case, there she was. Rick also told Mom that someone had ridden over to the next town to get the doctor and would bring him over as soon as he could.

Mom had given Robin some strong passionflower tea, which had helped her with the pain, and she was able to sleep a little between contractions. She was asleep when Skylar arrived, so Skylar sat on the back porch and talked to me for a while. She kept hugging me close and saying she couldn't believe I'd been in a battle that morning.

She also said something that made me very happy. She said she never wanted to leave me again, and that gave me an idea for a Christmas present for her.

Robin woke up then and called for Skylar, and I didn't see her again until the sun set that evening, when she came down to get something to eat. Mom was up with Robin, whose moans were getting even louder. Sometimes she would start to scream, and then it would be cut off abruptly like someone had kicked her in the stomach and knocked the air out of her. Mom told me earlier that the contractions were doing just that – knocking the air right out of her. Granny and Gram made us all a nice dinner, even though we found it hard to even taste it, knowing what Robin was going through.

After we ate, Skylar and I went out on the back porch again. The weather was unusually warm and it was a nice break to sit out there, even if we could still hear Robin's cries. We decided to take a walk out to see the horses and, as we walked, we talked about having kids. Frankly, neither of us was too excited to have any at that point, seeing how hard it was on Robin.

We noticed the eerie glow of an Aurora Borealis gaining strength in the northern sky while we watched the horses, and we wondered if there had been another solar superstorm to cause it. Not that it mattered anymore. There were no more power grids to take down, at least not in our part of the country. The only thing we had to worry about now, according to the National Guardsmen that had visited us in the spring, was increased radiation in the atmosphere, but that didn't feel like much of a risk after what we'd been through today. It was just an intangible, colorless, odorless "thing" in the air.

As we were walking back to the house, hand in hand, we heard Robin let out a blood-curdling scream. We looked at each other, and then started running. When we burst into the house, Alex was hollering down the stairs, "The baby's coming! Hurry!"

Skylar ran directly up the stairs, but I

stayed in the living room. I'd always thought it was just an urban legend that you needed to boil water for a birth, but Granny took a kettle of boiling water and poured it into a tub and set it aside to cool. When I asked her what it was for, she said that it was to wash the baby off after it came out. Gram piled my arms up with fluffy towels and sheets and told me to take them upstairs. I didn't want to go up there with all the blood and who knew what else, but she shooed me off toward the stairs and I didn't really have a choice.

When I got to the room, Mom said, "Good, Bracken, we need your help."

I almost fainted when I saw blood on the floor under Robin's legs. Robin was half-standing, with Alex on one side of her, holding her up, and Skylar on the other side. Robin had her nightgown pulled up over her huge belly but, thankfully, the way she was leaning over made it so I couldn't see the baby or anything. I could tell that Skylar wasn't quite strong enough to support Robin, so I took her place after laying the towels on a chair near Mom. Mom was kneeling on the floor in front of Robin, and Skylar knelt down beside her. Mom grabbed a towel and laid it in on the floor under

Robin, and then another one, which she draped over her arms.

"I see the head!" Mom said excitedly. "Keep pushing, honey, you're doing great."

"Where's the gawdamned doctor?" Alex yelled and Mom gave him a withering look.

"This baby's not going to wait for the doctor, Alex," she murmured. "Robin's doing just fine without him. Okay, honey, now push again."

Another contraction hit Robin like a bull kicking her in the stomach. I wondered if she thought about her dad then, and if she could identify now with the pain her dad must have felt before he died. As the pain died down, Robin's body sagged between Alex and me and I thought she might have passed out, but another contraction hit within a few seconds, and she straightened up and started pushing again.

I don't know how she could stand it. The contractions were so strong and she could barely catch her breath between each of them, let alone make any noise. The moaning and screaming from before was gone now, replaced with a cycle of bearing down, then almost passing out breathlessly. This went on for a long time; it felt like hours.

At one point, my arms were aching so

badly that it was all I could do to keep from dropping her. That was when Dad came to relieve me. He first tried to take Alex's place, but Alex just shook his head and stayed by his wife's side. I was really proud of my big brother then, for his strength and his devotion to his wife and baby.

I started to leave, but Mom said to stay, she might need me. I took a seat at the side of the room, as far away as I could get, which wasn't too easy in a room as crowded as that one was. I could tell by Mom's face that she was beginning to worry and at one point, she said, "I think the head may be stuck. I may have to make an incision."

I myself almost passed out at that, but Robin just nodded. Mom picked up her pair of sewing scissors, the ones she uses to snip threads, and poured some alcohol over them. She paused and took a deep breath before doing what she had to.

After that, things went pretty fast. Mom said, "Here it comes!" and Robin gave a big push. Next thing I knew, Mom was holding the baby in the towel, still connected to Robin by the umbilical cord. Robin slumped back toward the bed and Dad and Alex laid her gently on it, her legs still hanging off the end.

"It's a boy!" Skylar said exuberantly and, for the first time in what seemed like an eternity, Alex and Robin both smiled weakly.

Alex kissed his wife tenderly and pushed some pillows up under her head and back so she could half sit up. Mom laid the baby on Robin's partially flattened belly and Robin put a shaky hand on his head. For a moment, she just stared at him with happy tears in her eyes. Then it seemed another contraction hit her, because she stiffened up and Mom quickly handed the baby to Alex. It was so funny; Alex was so surprised, he almost dropped the baby, but he recovered in time and held him, all bloody and gooey, up to his cheek.

I thought the drama would be over since the baby was already born, but Mom said that she still needed to deliver the afterbirth. Just the sound of that alone made me want to head for the hills, but Mom had a job for me.

She told me to grab two spring clamps that I recognized from our workbench in the barn, and even though they'd already been sterilized, she had me pour alcohol over them again. Then, she told me to clamp them onto the umbilical cord about two inches apart from each other while she sterilized the large pair of shears we use for trimming the horses. She offered them to me to cut the cord, but I refused in the midst of my wooziness, and she ended up doing the job. I had to get away fast when Robin had another contraction and the afterbirth came gushing out. I did almost faint then and had to sit down fast, while Skylar laughed at me.

Skylar helped Mom clean up the floor, the sheets, and Robin, and the grandmas came up with the wash basin, the water in which had had to be heated up again, and gently washed the baby while he mewed like a newborn kitten.

The baby never cried out loud like most newborns, but you could tell by his beautiful pink coloring that he was healthy. After he was bathed, Granny put one of his diapers and a warm flannel gown on him and gave him to Robin. She was exhausted, but holding the baby seemed to give her new life, and she and Alex smiled and cooed over him. We all left the room then and let them have some time alone with their new son.

About an hour later, just after midnight, the doctor finally showed up. He explained that he had been held up treating the wounds of the marauders, some of which were quite serious. He had almost lost one who had a bullet lodged near his heart, but he was stable when the doctor finally left to come here. He went right up to Robin's room and checked on mother and son, cutting the baby's umbilical cord shorter and attaching a special clamp to it. He also weighed the baby and took measurements.

When he came back downstairs, he congratulated us, especially Mom, for a job well done, and told us that the baby had an unusually large head, which was probably why Robin had had so much trouble pushing him out. Other than that, the baby was perfectly healthy and he had every reason to believe that Robin would recover nicely.

Before we went to bed that night, or should I say early the next morning, we stopped by Robin and Alex's room to see the baby one last time. He had just finished nursing and was sleeping so angelically in Robin's arms, it seemed almost like it was a Hollywood movie.

Mom asked if they'd thought of a name for him yet and Alex looked Robin in the eyes for a few seconds before saying, in a husky sort of voice, "We're naming him John Joseph, after both his grandpas. We'll call him Joey." No one was more moved by the name than Dad, who was one of the namesakes.

When we were all ready to go to bed, I gave Skylar a kiss goodnight, then I lingered a little while after the others. I shook Alex's hand and he hugged me to him, saying, "Thanks for your help there, Buddy."

I kissed Robin's forehead and stroked my little nephew's downy soft head and finally went to bed.

Chapter 22

That Christmas was special for several reasons. We had survived our second (and hopefully last) marauder attack, our farm was prospering, we had completely adjusted to life without electricity and were even enjoying it, the newest addition to our family was a joy to everyone, and most importantly, to me anyway, I asked Skylar to be my wife.

First, let me tell you about what ended up happening to the bad guys. Rick Thomas and some of our other neighbors took them into town. It took them nearly seven hours to get there and by that time, many of them were nearly dead from exhaustion, injuries, and lack of food. Our guys made sure they stopped to let their captives get drinks from creeks and take breaks every now and then, but it was still quite an ordeal for them.

When they got to town, the town policeman and the county sheriff took over. Someone had ridden ahead to the next town to fetch the doctor, like I mentioned before, and he came and spent most of the evening trying to patch them up. About a half dozen of the ones who had gotten away were caught trying to steal from other farmers, all of whom were prepared for them thanks to the Fab Four; but there were others – no one knew how many – who were unaccounted for. The prisoners were all kept in the school gym and given food and blankets to sleep on, which was more than they deserved, if you ask me.

The sheriff was able to get a hold of the National Guard by short-wave radio and, the next day, an army transport came and picked up the marauders. The last we heard, they were to be taken to a larger county jail and we may have to travel there to testify at their trials. We don't know for sure at this point, though, because we are still under martial law and the regular courts are backed up so far, they may never catch up.

Things got back to normal pretty quickly for our family. Papa's head injury bled quite a bit the first couple of days, but had healed up enough by Christmas that he got his bandages removed and didn't have to pretend to be one of the shepherds in the nativity anymore. Dad, Calvin, and I finished getting the house and yard back to normal, except for the broken panes of glass. We didn't have any glass to replace them, so we just boarded up those empty spaces.

Little Joey is so incredible. I've never

been one to ooh and ahh over babies much, but there is just something so special about that kid. At just a week old, he'd look at each of us like he already recognized us, and he'd smile at us; really smile, not just gas, as some people like to claim. He rolled over from his tummy to his back at just five days old and we had to watch him carefully whenever we laid him on a bed or the couch after that. Besides having an uncommonly large head (which to me doesn't seem much bigger than most babies I've seen), he seems to be unusually strong and smart.

Now, at just five months old, he can already sit up and say a few words: mama, dada, papa, and nus (for nurse, which he likes to do quite often). Mom says that he is quite young to be doing those things and even I, who have no experience with babies, can tell he looks too young to be so developed.

And he has so much personality! He loves to play hide and seek and can always figure out where you've hidden his toy right away. When he finds it, he starts giggling so loudly and happily, you can't help but laugh, too.

Every time I come into the room that he's in, he gets excited and stretches out his arms for me to pick him up. He always says something that sounds like "banban" when he sees me and Robin thinks he's trying to say Bracken. He doesn't say anything to Calvin yet and that makes Calvin kind of jealous, but Robin says that Calvin is just harder to say. He calls Mom and the grandmas "mama," as well as his mom, and he calls Dad and Papa both "papa." Robin says he'll sort all that out later. Anyway, he is a joy to us all and we only wish there were more of him to share.

I know you probably can't wait to read about how I proposed to Skylar. Well, first I have to tell you all I had to do to prepare for the actual proposal. The day after Joey's birth, I took Skylar back to town. I spent all afternoon trying to get Mr. and Mrs. Tipton – I mean Dave and Barb – alone so I could tell them my intention and ask for their blessing. They surprised me by saying that they couldn't imagine a better son-in-law. I think Skylar got a little suspicious when she came into the room and found us all hugging with big smiles on our faces.

Next, I had to find a ring. Mom had given Alex (for Robin) an antique wedding and engagement ring set that her grandmother had given her before she died. Mom offered to let me have her wedding set, but I didn't want to take them from her, so I asked Granny if she had something for me. Granny had tears in her eyes when she took off her wedding rings, which she had continued to wear even fifteen years after Grandpa's death, and told me that she would be honored to have Skylar and me carry on the love that she and Grandpa had had for each other by wearing their rings. She even got out Grandpa's ring from her treasure box and gave it to me to wear.

Granny's engagement ring isn't just the usual white-diamond-in-a-gold-band type. It has a light blue, heart-shaped gem, which Granny said is topaz, set in a silver filigree band, and the wedding ring is a band of tiny diamonds also set in silver filigree, which is designed to fit snug against the engagement band. I knew Skylar would love it, because her favorite color is blue and she likes silver jewelry better than gold.

On Christmas Eve I rode to town to pick up Skylar, as her parents and I had arranged. Mom sent them a big, juicy ham and Barb had baked us a sweet potato pie. I'm sure Skylar got suspicious again when her mother hugged her tight and had tears in her eyes when she said goodbye, because she asked me on the way back home what was up. I said it was nothing special, just another wonderful Christmas with the most beautiful girl in the world. I can be romantic when I really try.

That evening we had a meal that included a wild turkey I had shot a few days before, and then we headed to the church for the Christmas Eve candlelight service. The parking lot was filled with horses and wagons of all types, many of them homemade from old tractor and truck parts like the Banks's. The funniest and most ironic contraption was a small horse trailer rigged up to be pulled by two horses, with the people riding inside the trailer and being pulled by the horses instead of the other way around. We all got a good laugh out of that one.

Everyone was really surprised, though, when an old truck came chugging in and Jim Riley, one of the mechanics in town, got out. We all swarmed his truck while he told us how he had been working on converting the vehicle to burn corn and soybean oil instead of gasoline. He said he could also convert an older model automobile to burn wood if anyone was interested. Several of the men, including Dad, Calvin, and I, were interested in finding out how to do it and we stood around for a good half hour, talking about it while the women cooed over little Joey until Reverend Campbell called everyone in for the service.

After the service, we talked to Mr. Andresen for a little while and he said that there had been another solar flare on the 17th, just as I'd thought. He said it was unprecedented, as far as any scientists knew, to have so many CME's in a row. He was a little worried about excess radiation affecting people, animals, and even plants, and he warned us to watch out for signs of radiation sickness, like nausea and vomiting, spontaneous bleeding, blisters and ulcers, severe weakness, and hair loss. He also said that radiation can cause all sorts of birth defects and we breathed a sigh of relief that little Joey seemed to be normal – well, except for his unusual head size, intelligence, and strength, that is.

When we got home from church, we all had a mug of warm milk and some cookies that Gram had made, and then everyone went to bed. Everyone except me, that is. I had told Mom and Dad about the proposal, so they didn't mind that I stayed downstairs with Skylar. They were real happy about it, too, which surprised me, because I thought they would give me the whole "you're only seventeen" speech. I guess they were happy about the way Alex and Robin's marriage had worked out and they realized that we'd be eighteen in a few months anyway *and* they were already so used to having Skylar around. I think they also appreciated the fact that I hadn't just sprung it on them like Alex did, so they were more prepared to get their heads around it.

I made Skylar sit in the armchair right beside the Christmas tree and I knelt down in front of her. I know it was a really old-fashioned way of doing it, but it just felt right, with the old-fashioned way we were living now. Skylar started to cry before I even asked her, and when I did, she threw her arms around me and said yes before I could show her the ring. Just as I thought, she loved the ring, and I mean *loved* it. She put it on right away and even though it was a little big, she wouldn't take it off, but just kept looking at it and hugging me over and over. I didn't show her the matching wedding band. I wanted to surprise her with that on our wedding day. See? I told you I could be romantic when I tried.

We stayed up almost all night and cuddled together in a blanket in front of the fire, talking about the future. We talked about the wedding and where we would live afterwards and how many children we wanted. Even though I was scared to death at the thought of seeing Skylar go through what Robin had, I had to admit I'd love to have a little tyke like Joey. Of course, Skylar was all for having a dozen kids – she loves kids.

We decide that we'd live with Mom and Dad, if that was okay with them, because Robin and Alex were talking about moving to Robin's old house. We all hated that idea of course, especially since they'd be taking Joey with them, but we understood that they needed more room and a home of their own now that they had a family. Alex was excited to try his hand at cattle ranching and joked that we'd have to start calling him the Baron, and that he'd even give us a job helping him if we were nice enough. Robin wasn't too keen on keeping a bull again since her Dad's accident, but Alex said they'd leave it with the Jenkins's and borrow it as needed.

On Christmas morning, all the women gathered around Skylar to see the ring, and Granny showed her how to tie a little piece of cloth around the underside of the ring to make it fit. Then, we had a nice breakfast of bacon, eggs, and toast made from Mom's fresh-baked bread, along with some home-made cinnamon rolls made by Gram. We gathered around the Christmas tree and sang carols and exchanged gifts. I won't say what everyone got, but I will mention some of the more memorable gifts.

Dad had taken the electric washing machine and refashioned it so it could be agitated manually or by riding a stationary bike. That way, Mom could get her exercise while doing laundry, he joked. But more importantly, the tub could be filled automatically with heated water from the solar water heater, pumped through the pipes by the hydraulic pump, and then, at the flick of a lever, could drain out through the existing drainage pipes. No more filling and dumping, filling and dumping. The clothes still had to be wrung through the rollers, but Dad had mounted them on top of the washer so they could swing over the tub when it was time to wring out the clothes. Dad said he'd work on some kind of solar dryer for her next Christmas and Mom laughed and said that it seemed laundry was becoming a theme for gifts for her.

One of my favorite gifts – besides Skylar agreeing to be my wife, of course – was from Calvin. He had taken apart an old so-lar-powered model car he had built for his fourth grade science fair project and had rigged up a way to recharge batteries with it. He had gathered up our dead rechargeable batteries, recharged them all, and then gave them to us in some of our long-forgotten gadgets, like flashlights, clocks, and our Nintendo DS.

My favorite was my MP3 player. I had almost forgotten how nice music sounded. Skylar and I spent the rest of the day just lis-tening to music from before PF Day. Little Joey's eyes got real big when I put the headphones up to his ears and we all had a good laugh about that.

Skylar spent New Year's Eve with us, too. We had a wonderful night, lounging outside around the fire pit because the weather was still so nice. In fact, the weather never did get cold that winter. We had a week in February where the temperature dropped just a few degrees below freezing, just enough to freeze the water in our buck-ets for our cold cellar, but other than that, it stayed in the fifties and sixties most of the time. Mr. Andresen said that was most likely because of the increased sun activity. It made the winter very enjoyable, whatever the cause was.

In March and April, Skylar and I helped Alex and Robin work on Robin's old place to get it ready to move into this summer. Nobody had lived there for over two years and it was not set up for living in without electricity like our house is. The fences had to be fixed for holding cattle again and the barn filled with hay for feed and fresh straw for calving. Sometimes Mom, Dad, and Calvin came along and helped, too. Little Joey sat and watched all the activity with great interest and sometimes would clap and giggle when we were concentrating real hard on some task and we'd all end up laughing and taking a break. I'll tell you, that kid was the best manager anyone could ask for.

Two weeks ago, I turned eighteen and Mom said I was officially graduated from school. Skylar turned eighteen just three days ago and we had a very special birthday party for her at the diner with her parents and lots of friends from town. Jenny and Ben were there, although Jenny had broken up with Ben and was now dating his friend, Matt. Ben was interested in Taylor Smith, Irvine's little sister. I wanted to warn him against getting too involved with that family, but Skylar told me to let it alone.

After the party, Skylar and I sat outside in back and I remembered her words to me two and a half years ago like it was just yesterday: "nothing is ever going to be the same from this day forward."

Tonight, as I sit here writing the final words of my story about learning how to survive in a world without electricity, and how to survive cowboy-style battles and pioneer-type emergencies, I realize that I've become accustomed to writing with a pen on paper. My handwriting has actually improved a great deal, and probably my grammar, too. All in all, I think PF Day has been a wonderful gift to my family and me, and I can only feel grateful to the sun for giving us this new life. I know we are stronger and closer than ever and are prepared to survive whatever may come our way.

And now comes the most important event of my life, as I wait here in the living room, surrounded by my family and friends, for my beautiful bride to come down the stairs and become my wife.

Discussion questions

1. Immediately after the students in Bracken's class heard the initial big explosion on PF Day, what did they fear had happened?

2. Why didn't Bracken know Skylar very well, even though they had known each other almost all their lives? How is it possible to feel you know someone without really knowing him or her?

3. What things did Bracken's family already have that gave them an advantage for survival after PF Day? (Examples: fireplace, harvested grain, hunting equipment, water well, chickens etc.)

4. What things did they acquire that aided their survival? (Examples: livestock, wood-burning stove, horse-drawn farming equipment, etc.)

5. What things did they make to aid their survival? (Examples: solar bottle light, solar water heater, solar heat exchangers, etc.)

6. How did the townspeople pull together to help each other survive? (Examples: town market, stoves made from old water heaters, specialization and trading of skills, etc.)

7. What were some of the long-term consequences of PF Day for society in terms of physical, emotional, and financial problems? (Examples: millions of deaths, post-traumatic stress, financial meltdown, etc.)

8. How did Bracken, Alex, and Calvin change throughout the story? What specific things made you aware of those changes?

9. How did Bracken and his family perceive Ben's personality while he stayed with them?

10. How did the presence of Bracken's grandparents help the family?

11. How did the death of Robin's dad, the near-fatal appendicitis of the little boy in town, and Robin's difficult childbirth affect Bracken's mom's confidence in her medical knowledge?

12. What did people speculate about baby Joey's unusually large head and intelligence?

Questions and Answers

How likely is a solar superstorm like the one in the book to happen?

The story portrays a "perfect storm" scenario, so it is unlikely but still a possibility. There are solar events happening every year and some are quite large, but not only does the CME (Coronal Mass Ejection) have to be huge and highly charged magnetically, it has to hit the Earth's atmosphere just right in order to cause the kind of destruction portrayed in the story. The CME itself rotates, one side being positively charged and the other being negatively charged. If the CME hits Earth's atmosphere with the same polarity, positive-to-positive or negative-to-negative, the CME pulse will be repelled into space, much like what happens when you hold two magnets together with the same poles facing each other. But if it hits the opposite polarity, and the CME's magnetic field is strong enough, the Earth's magnetic field may collapse and the surge will quickly circumnavigate the globe, likely taking down most, if not all, of the power grids and short-circuiting a large percentage of all electronic devices. There are only a few places in the world that manufacture the 125 kilowatt transformers that are the backbone of the power grids; if a majority of those transformers are fried, it could take years, maybe even decades, to replace them.

What would be the greatest dilemma for humans if something like this were to happen?

It would be hard to pinpoint one problem that would be the greatest, since so many things would most likely cause millions and maybe even billions of deaths. Immediately with the electromagnetic surge, up to two thirds of vehicles on the road would experience engine stall and traffic lights would blink off, causing a multitude of traffic accidents. Some people might be electrocuted by surges through the power lines and electronic devices, and workers at power plants may die in the explosion of transformers. Within a few days, people who rely on ventilators, dialysis machines, and other electronic devices would probably die as the fuel for the back-up generators runs out. Pharmaceutical companies would run out of supplies of medicines and within a few months, people who rely on medicines to stay alive may die. Remember, no manufacturing or drilling for and refining oil can occur without power. Food supplies will run low and many people will have to loot or fight for food. Sewage treatment plants will not be operable, so sewage will back up on city streets, causing all sorts of diseases; diseases for which medicine is no longer available to cure. Finding clean water will become a priority very quickly as cities will no longer be able to pump and treat water. Keeping warm will be a struggle in colder climates, as not that many people have heat sources that do not require electricity or fossil fuels to run.

Find Out More

"Our sun is approaching a period of high turbulence, referred to as the solar maximum, with many scientists suggesting a peak in activity around 2013." This activity could result in a solar superstorm, which, under the perfect circumstances, could cause the collapse of the power grid as portrayed in How I Became a Teenage Survivalist. Find out more about solar superstorms and coronal mass ejections (CMEs) by visiting:

NOVA Secrets of the Sun
http://www.pbs.org/wgbh/nova/space/
secrets-sun.html

The Sun's Wrath: Worst Solar Storms in History http://www.space.com/12584-worst-solar-storms-sun-flares-history.html

NASA Science: A Super Solar Flare
http://science.nasa.gov/science-news/
science-at-nasa/2008/06may_carrington
flare/

Learning how to survive without electricity is all about creative problem solving. Think about everything in your life that runs on electricity and try to figure out a way to replace each of them. The links below show how Bracken's family and friends solved some of their most pressing problems. Find out how to become a survivalist:

How to make pop bottle "light bulbs"
http://www.guardian.co.uk/enviroment/2011/dec/23/sunlight-bulbs-plastic-bottles-light#

How to make a homemade washing machine
http://www.off-grid.net/2010/04/22/diy-washing-machine-and-homemade-laundry-soap/

How to make a wood-burning stove from an old hot water heater
http://www.instructables.com/id/Convert-a-Hot-Water-Heater-Into-a-Wood-Stove/

How to make a hydraulic ram pump to pump water
http://www.instructables.com/id/Hydraulic-Ram-Pump/

A Message from the Author:

Thank you for taking the time to read my book. I would be honored if you would consider leaving a review for it on *Amazon*.

About the Author

Julie Casey lives in a rural area near St. Joseph, Missouri, with her husband, Jonn Casey, a science teacher, and their three youngest sons. After teaching preschool for fifteen years, she has been homeschooling her four sons for ten years. Julie has Bachelor of Science degrees in education and computer programming and has written four books. She enjoys historical reenacting, wildlife rehabilitation, teaching her children, and writing books that capture the imaginations of young people.

Find out more at www.julielcasey.com.

Acknowledgements

Thanks to the folks at the Office of Letters and Light for sponsoring the NaNoWriMo (National Novel Writing Month) contest during which this book was written. The motivation to write this book from start to finish in the month of November 2011 came from their inspirational and humorous emails. I encourage everyone to support this worthy cause through donations, and maybe even to try the writing challenge sometime.

A huge debt of gratitude is due to my lovely friend Landi Quinlin for editing the book and making insightful suggestions on how to make it better before I submitted it to the publisher. Big thanks and much love to the family and friends who read the manuscript and offered ideas and support, including, but not limited to, Jan Powell, Lee Powell, Myrna Hopkins, Amanda Eldridge, Sue Greffer, Jean Newton, Chyre Buntz, Vona Edwards, South Holt R-1 School students, and fellow authors Tracy Lane, Judy Pierce, Patricia Vanasse, Monica Strang, and Whitney Grady.

Big thanks and kudos to my pal Jim Conlon of Scout Productions for the creation of the fabulous trailer for the book, to John Morris for his keen camera work, Brad Boe for the awesome special effects, Phil Meyer for his marvelous narration, and to the kids, teachers, and parents at South Holt High School who starred in it, particularly Mac Kelly, Gavin Graupman, Hannah Smith, Macala Shirley, Jonn Casey, Landi Quinlin, and William Barton.

And finally, thanks to my dear husband Jonn Casey, my wonderful children and grandchildren, my loving parents and parents-in-law, and all my extended family and friends. Without you all, none of this would have been possible.

Check out these titles from
Amazing Things Press

Keeper of the Mountain by Nshan Erganian

Rare Blood Sect by Robert L. Justus

Evoloving by James Fly

Survival In the Kitchen by Sharon Boyle

Stop Beating the Dead Horse by Julie L. Casey

In Daddy's Hands by Julie L. Casey

Time Lost: Teenage Survivalist II by Julie L. Casey

Starlings by Jeff Foster

MariKay's Rainbow by Marilyn Weimer

Convolutions by Vashti Daise

Seeking the Green Flash by Lanny Daise

Nikki's Heart by Nona j. Moss

Nightmares or Memories by Nona j. Moss

Thought Control by Robert L. Justus

Palightte by James Fly

I, Eugenius by Larry W. Anderson

Check out these children's titles from
Amazing Things Press

The Boy Who Loved the Sky by Donna E. Hart

Terreben by Donna E. Hart

Sherry Strawberry's Clubhouse by Donna E. Hart

Finally Fall by Donna E. Hart

Thankful for Thanksgiving by Donna E. Hart

Make Room for Maggie by Donna E. Hart

Toddler Tales by Kathy Blair

A Cat Named Phyl by Donna E. Hart

Geography Studies with Animal Buddies by Vashti Daise

The Princess and the Pink Dragon by Thomas Kirschner

The Happy Butterfly by Donna E. Hart

Amazing Things Press

www.amazingthingspress.com

40157048R00147

Made in the USA
Lexington, KY
30 March 2015